Retribution

Anita Dotts

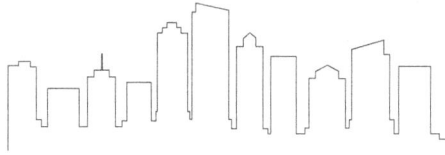

Chapter One
Sunday Night/Day 1 Monday

My phone is ringing, looking down at the number apprehensively, I answer the call, choking on my words. Taking too long to speak.

I hear the worry in Connor's voice. "Are you alright, Allory?" My brother asks.

God I'm not ready, I wish for titanium walls around my fear.

But rather than let him know I say, "I'm okay."

Ironically, the waiting is finally over. My heart is pounding trying to listen closely to what Connor is saying.

Blindly looking out the window, no longer seeing the splendor of the Marseille waterfront at dusk. I flash back to another waterfront etched on the back of my eyelids.

Acknowledging I'm choosing to face the monster again; I can't crumble in fear.

Hearing my brother Connor asking me again if I am okay.

"Just needed a minute Connor to get my thoughts together.

"Truly, I appreciate you handling everything.

"I can't wait to see you, Sean and Avery. I am grateful you are all meeting me at the airport. I will text you the time my flight arrives. See you soon. I love you."

Hearing Connor wishing me safe travels before hanging up.

For a moment just breathing, I hear the metaphoric clock ominously ticking inside my head.

Here begins night- to -day of this scary journey.

Unchaining the memories, I'm bombarded by questions I have faced twice before.

Am I strong enough to do this?

If don't do this, will I ever be safe again?

Sharing a flat with Céline, and counselling support helps to deal with my past, but knowing I would eventually face him again prevented true healing.

Steading my nerves, I watch the stars begin to twinkle in the darkened sky reflecting the lights of a bustling Marseille.

I reserve a seat for the seven-thirty TGV train from Marseille to Paris tonight. Booking a direct flight with Air France from Charles de Gaulle tomorrow morning at ten-ten am arriving at YVR in Vancouver at eleven ten am local time.

Procuring a room overnight at Gare de Lyon hotel for tonight makes it easy to get my flight in the morning.

Calling my boss Andre at home, I explain the need to go to Vancouver to deal with a complicated family matter. He reassures me that most of my current work can be done remotely while I am away.

I recall my conversation with Connor over two years ago. I remember thinking I couldn't wait to leave all the terrible things that had happened behind me. I was so excited to move to France and start anew.

"Allory did you hear what I said about needing full time security when you are in France," Connor asked. He'd looked so tired and worried. I feel bad, leaving him to manage everything because I needed distance from here to rebuild my life.

"I know someone in the city who runs a security firm with connections to France. I hired Jake to organize security for you.

"When Price gets a parole hearing, you will need to return to Vancouver."

At that moment, all I could think about was escaping from the recent traumatic events.

"You go to Paris. Sean, Avery, and I will visit when we can."

Even now the memory stirs my guilt for leaving my family to run away.

Wandering into my bedroom, I drag out my two carry-on packing only the essentials.

Céline breezes into our flat about a half hour after Connor's call turning on lights. Calling my name, noticing my luggage at the door.

"It's time, isn't it?" she sinks down next to me on the sofa.

"Yes, I made all the reservations for tonight and a flight to Vancouver in the morning. Andre was very understanding when I called."

Céline surrounds my face with her hands. "Right now, I am going to get you a glass of wine."

"Then I will drive you to the train." She walks into the kitchen getting wine glasses down from the cupboard and grabs the Chardonnay from the pantry.

We sit quietly sipping our wine. No words are needed between us.

Looking into Céline's eyes, I see her fear for me.

"Céline don't be scared. A security detail is following me to Vancouver. I'm staying in a condo with extra security when I arrive."

Wrapping my arm around her shoulders, I pull her close for a hug.

"We have been living the dream, Céline. Time to pay the Piper!

"Avery and the boys are meeting me at the airport when I arrive in Vancouver. I promise to text you when I get there."

Céline smiles through her tears as she knows my brothers and sister well from their frequent visits to Marseille.

Though I am traveling light, with just two small carry-ons, I think about what I packed trying to make sure I haven't forgotten anything important.

I can't believe I forgot to pack my laptop. I hurry back to my bedroom.

Glancing around the room, I spy the pictures of our trips around France hung on the wall, proof of a life in living colour.

Remembering the spring can be cool on the West Coast; I open the closet by the door to add my warmer coat to one of the carry-ons.

"Chérie," Céline calls me from the kitchen. "You ready to leave for the train station?"

"Yes," I say coming into the kitchen to grab my purse from the counter.

I slide my laptop into my briefcase and my purse in the outside pocket for easy access. I collect my luggage at the door.

"What do you want me to tell everyone after you're gone?"

"Just tell them I went home to see my family."

Céline drives me to the train station for seven fifteen pm as there is a bit of walk to the train itself. She hugs me tightly with tears in her eyes.

"Allory, call or text me when you can about how things are going."

I hug her for a moment longer holding back my tears.

"I will call or text you when I land in Vancouver."

Picking up my luggage, I walk toward the thruway to board the train.

The evening train from Vieux Port has fewer stops than the day train before reaching Paris. It is comfortable but I am too wired to do more than rest for the three and half hours to Paris.

The train arrives in Paris at ten thirty-five pm. The train station is less crowded but still people are coming and going.

Making my way to the street exit, the Gare de Lyon hotel is just a two-minute walk from the station. I'll be able to get up early to easily make my flight at Charles de Gaulle in the morning.

When I reach the front desk; check in is completed quickly and I take the elevator to the second floor. Unlocking the door to my room; suddenly I am exhausted. I set my alarm for six am to grab breakfast and get the train to the airport.

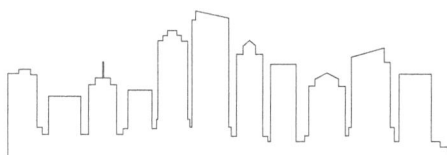

Chapter Two
Monday Day one

The next morning, the train is packed going to Charles de Gaulle Airport. I check in for my flight on my cell phone.

The airport security is straightforward. I line up for the bus that will take us to our aircraft. As I board the plane it is raining.

I already miss the sun in the south of France.

I'll be in Vancouver in just over ten hours knowing the time change will be brutal.

I don't want to be exhausted when I arrive in Vancouver. I take my e-book out to read for the first few hours.

Hours of the droning from the aircraft helps me fall asleep.

Waking suddenly in the darkened cabin, panicked before I remember,

I'm on the plane.

Taking a few deep breaths, the silent question persists, can I face my abuser again?

The parole hearing is going to be my first hurtle on Tuesday morning.

I wake slowly as we make our descent into Vancouver. We left Paris at ten am and with the flight almost ten hours and time difference, I'm landing in Vancouver at eleven am local time.

It is cloudy, cool, and rainy as expected for early spring. I see white capped mountains during our descent to the airport. People were likely getting in spring skiing today.

I clear Customs with no problems.

Having only carry-on luggage, I go directly to the arrival area where Avery, Sean and Connor will meet me.

Happily, I see my siblings' smiling faces in the crowded arrival area. My sister Avery sees me first and pushes to the front to give me a big hug.

Connor and Sean stand back to wait their turn. When Avery lets me go, Sean wraps his arms tight around me like he doesn't want to let me go.

Connor taps him on the shoulder. "My turn," he interrupts dryly while tugging me towards him I feel safer in the refuge of his arms.

Avery slips her arm around my shoulders as we weave our way through the crowd toward the exit. My brothers follow behind with my luggage.

"We are so glad to see you!" Avery is smiling at the same time tears are running down her cheeks. I turn to brush them away.

"Those better be happy tears!" I scold her.

Exiting from Arrivals to the parkade, Connor is parked a short distance away. Sean stows my luggage in the trunk before getting in the front seat with Connor. Avery and I climb into the back.

Driving out of the parkade, Connor follows the traffic into the city.

Avery turns in her seat to face me. "I am glad you are here I just wish it was for a happy occasion instead of facing Leon Price at his parole hearing tomorrow.

"The condo I rented for us has plenty of room for our needs. It is a short walk to Stanley Park."

"Avery, I know all the arrangements you made for my stay will be superb!" Giving her hand a squeeze.

We cross several bridges over the Fraser River. A multitude of neighbour-hoods' flash by during the drive.

We reach the condo building on Georgia Street in just under an hour.

Avery leads us to the main floor of condo building because we need to sign in with the concierge to receive elevator access and parking passes.

The penthouse is on the eighty-eighth floor with the elevator opening into the entrance of the suite.

Walking into the living room, my glance lingering on the view from the windows of the harbour and deep green forest of Stanley Park.

Feeling nostalgic seeing the majestic North Shore Mountains with towering views reaching into a clear blue sky.

I spy a seaplane above Lions Gate Bridge getting ready to land in the harbour nearby. It forces me to remember that despite past trauma I still love Vancouver even if I don't ever want to live here permanently again.

Curious to see the condo's layout I wander through the main floor spying a kitchen, pantry, dining area.

There are two bedrooms on the main floor with a master bedroom and ensuite on the second floor.

"Wow Avery, did you plan to have a small army stay here with me?"

"No, just us and the security team that will protect you while you are in Vancouver," Avery grins.

For the first time since Connor's call yesterday, I breathe deeply relaxing my tight muscles. Relieved the security in the building is tight.

The open design of the condo prevents me feeling penned in. Most importantly I am not alone because my brothers and sister stand with me just like last time after Price terrorized me.

I grab my luggage by the hallway table after toeing off my shoes.

Walking into the living rooms, I see Avery, Sean, and Connor reclining on the sofa. I can't avoid a big yawn.

"I really need a nap as I am still on French time. What are your plans for the rest of the day?"

Avery glances at Connor, "I'm staying here today, as I can work remotely while the boys go back to work, returning for dinner."

"Sean has agreed to cook if I order a grocery delivery."

"Thanks, sounds great, yawning I head upstairs.

Opening my luggage, I pull out my pajamas leaving my crumpled clothes on the floor, I climb in bed, asleep in minutes.

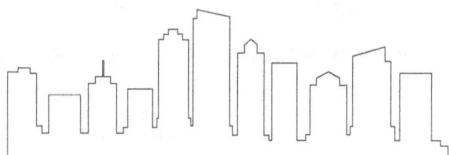

Chapter Three

After leaving the condo, Connor drops Sean at his truck. The traffic is light as he makes his way to his office.

Taking a shortcut to the stairwell, He jogs up the stairs to his office on the fourth floor barely winded. He waves to his secretary in passing.

Settled behind his desk, he turns on his computer, opening a brief he is working on.

It is hard to stay focused, he worries how Allory will face her abuser tomorrow at the parole hearing. How can seeing him not re-traumatize her again!

Connor grinds his teeth, feeling powerless. He can only stand with her at the hearing tomorrow, unsure that is enough.

Leon Price ironically was acquainted with our family. He was always a cunning competitor in business. His brutal side carefully hidden.

After he sexually assaulted Allory; he continued to prey on her.

Stubbornly, she came to court every day to ensure Price went to prison for sexually assaulting her as there was not enough evidence to convict him for more serious crimes.

Connor sets to work on finishing his brief before his next client appointment.

Driving home at the end of his workday, he plans to shower and change before going to the condo for dinner with his family. His cell rings.

Picking up the call on hands free. "Hey, Jake"

"Connor, the condo security has been in place since early this morning before Allory arrived. Her French detail took a return flight home.

"How is Allory doing?"

"After we arrived at the condo she went for a nap. Avery is working remotely to be able to keep her company when she wakes up."

"I'm planning to come by the condo later in the day to check in and introduce Allory to Angel and Marc. See you then." Jake hangs up.

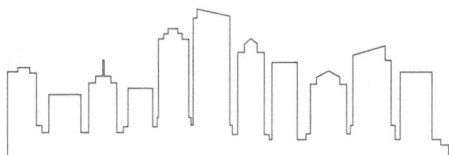

Chapter Four
Day One to night

Avery goes upstairs, peeking around the bedroom door to see if Allory is still sleeping.

She is lying facing the door in a deep sleep. I am glad she is home but worry about tomorrow.

How many other sexually assaulted women must face their abuser a second time?

Returning downstairs, Avery completes final instructions she emails to her staff. Her intern will manage the new designs projects, knowing to connect with me if she reaches a snag.

Avery thinks back to when Price had personal and business dealings with her family.

The long-ago conversation with my parents about Allory's sexual assault pops into her head. Remembering when they denied any possibility that Price could have assaulted her in their home.

When DNA evidence confirmed he was Allory's rapist, I believe the parents couldn't live with the fact that my sister had been abused in their home by a man they did business with.

They sold the house and moved to Portugal with the excuse that Vancouver weather was too cold, and they wanted to live in the sunshine. They avoided any repercussions for having business dealings with him.

Connor keeps in touch with them, but they have never come back to Vancouver since the move.

We had no idea that Price was guilty of worse crimes until he ordered Allory's abduction while he was awaiting his rape trial. He tried to ship her to Asia to be a sex slave!

It was my baby sister who rescued herself from the traffickers. She has been so strong and brave but after all she has gone through it has marked her deeply.

Allory's experiences impacted me and my brothers differently.

Having a firsthand experience seeing the evidence of how Price brutalized her, as a woman it shook me to the core.

Sean has been quieter and angry after the trial; opposed to Connor who stayed keenly focused on Allory's safety.

Our world view became darker and scarier after her rape and almost being sold into slavery. We have chosen to stick together to ensure we are there for each other and Allory.

Leon Price is escorted by the prison guard to a meeting room where he can talk with his lawyer. He is dressed in a red t-shirt, sweatshirt and pants made through the prison tailoring work program.

He is a tall, muscular man with dark brown eyes and hair. His demeanor is darker, ominous in silence, his gaze laser focused.

His lawyer is here to discuss the parole hearing tomorrow.

Leon turns his penetrating stare at his lawyer. The man seems to be sweating but pulls some documents out of his briefcase. He outlines the parole hearing process for tomorrow, his release date and conditions of his parole.

As his lawyer drones on, Leon smiles inside knowing he has purposefully been a hassle-free inmate with exemplary behaviour during served time. He made sure there would be positive reports from the prison social worker and other personnel.

"Do you have any questions about the parole process before I go, Mr. Price?"

"No, I will see you tomorrow at the hearing."

Leon is amused at his lawyer's discomfort but satisfied that he is almost guaranteed parole tomorrow.

Avoiding Leon's gaze, his lawyer shoves his papers into his briefcase and silently leaves the room.

The guard takes him back to his cell. Lying on his bunk, Leon begins planning what he will do to Allory once he gets out. He will be on parole which means he can't have any contact with her. He has no intention of letting that girl escape him this time. He has spent most of his time inside planning his revenge. With that thought his mouth stretches into a nasty smile.

Later in the afternoon, Leon is in the visitor room meeting with his second in command Luis.

"Allory arrived this morning from Paris. She and her siblings are staying in a condo on Georgia with tight security. We will have to wait until she leaves the condo to target her," explains Luis.

Leon gives Luis instructions, "Set up surveillance and follow her whenever she leaves the condo. Give me daily reports of who she sees, where she goes and how her security responds when your men get close.

"She is going to pay for putting me in prison. I expect to be out of this joint by Friday.

"How is the planning for the next auction coming for Saturday. Do we have enough merchandise to sell?"

"Yes, the merchandise is being housed at the warehouse, ready for sale at the auction. Plans are set to get the shipment from the warehouse after the auction to the container we have at the docks."

Luis stands to leave. "Talk with you after the hearing tomorrow."

Again, Leon is escorted back to his cell. He stretches out on the cot tucking his hands behind his head. He entertains himself planning how he will make Allory pay for his prison stay.

Luis returns to Vancouver and calls a meeting with all known associates for seven pm tonight. He wants more eyes and ears on Allory's movements starting later tonight.

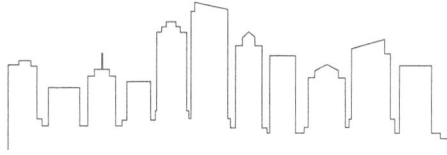

Chapter Five

Once home, Connor showers, changes into jeans and a t-shirt. He mulls over his conversation with Sean two days ago.

"Connor, I'm worried about balancing my new work projects with time for Allory.

"I'm also concerned how Allory will manage seeing Price at the parole hearing."

Reminding Sean that Avery and I would be there to support Allory too didn't seem to alleviate his worries.

Realizing at the time, there was more going on with Sean, I needed to make time to talk with him about it.

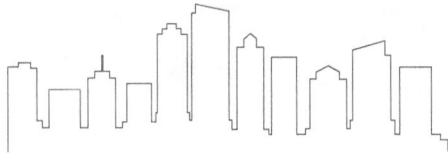

Chapter Six

I'm surprised I slept so deeply after the flight. Stepping into the glassed covered shower as opposed to the oval tub I will try it out when I want a long soak.

After showering I dress in jeans and loose red sweater as Vancouver weather in March is often chilly and windy.

The condo is quiet, with the faint swish of traffic rising from the street below.

Putting on soft music to play in the background as I unpack my carry-ons putting my clothing in the dresser next to the bed. I will likely borrow some of Avery's fancier clothes while I am here.

There is a study hidden in an alcove next to the window I leave my laptop and cell phone on the desk.

A glimpse of scenic Stanley Park; a deep green forest surrounded by ocean. The view reminds me, it used to be my favorite place, with its seawall, aquarium and miniature train.

I see Avery diligently working on her computer when I come downstairs.

She looks up from her screen. "How did you sleep?"

"Slept like a log!"

"Give me ten minutes to complete this last bit of work, Allory."

"Are you hungry?"

"Starving like a wild animal. Have the groceries you ordered arrived?"

"Yes, I put everything away in the fridge and cupboards.

"Why don't you make us a snack, and tea. I will join you when I finish this last email," Avery suggests.

Boiling the water to make tea, I set out teacups, cream and sugar. I'm arranging cut up fruit on a platter when Avery comes into the kitchen, sitting down on a stool at the counter.

"Wow, it is nice to have someone fix me a snack, Allory!"

We chat casually, bringing each other up-to-date on our lives. I miss this closeness with my sister.

Connor and Sean arrive, already vetted by downstairs security when we got our elevator passes.

"Hello brothers. You both clean up nice," teases Avery.

The boys preen for us, we burst out laughing. In that moment aware how much I have missed my family.

Realizing I practically slept the day away. We move to the comfortable seating in the living room, needing to turn on lighting as it's dark outside.

Hating to bring the mood down, I needed details about the parole hearing in the morning.

I turn to face Connor sitting to my right. "Tell me about the hearing tomorrow."

Frowning, Connor leans forward in his seat.

"It is almost certain that he will get parole. From my discreet enquiries, it seems he has been a model inmate while continuing to manage his business empire while incarcerated.

"Price has not forgotten for a moment that you put him in prison. His priorities when released will be to deal with you while retaking full control over his legal and illegal business empire.

"Jake, at my request has done a thorough investigation into Price's operations both legal and illegal. He is a powerful man with a lot of friends in high places."

We are quiet for a moment, assimilating Connor's words.

I can guess what my family are thinking. At this point they would be happier if I hide away from Price forever!

Knowing that hiding won't work. I'm confident Price has the resources to find me wherever I go. Hiding would be a win for Price; I'd be without my family and friends' support.

I interrupt the prolonged silence. "You three stand with me and I believe Jake will protect me while we wait for Price to be paroled. I don't think Price realizes we plan to turn the tables on him."

I think to myself; when he has me abducted, he may not seriously harm me to the point he can't sell me to a foreign buyer. I doubt Price will underestimate me again.

I take a moment to make eye contact with Avery, then Sean and finally Connor.

I take a deep breath. "I am all in Connor," I say fiercely.

"This time I want to ensure he gets charged for trafficking and imprisoned for life.

"I need to sit in on that hearing tomorrow to confirm I am back in Vancouver. I willingly accept further outings to throw my defiance in his face."

Connor leans back with an arm over the sofa, scrutinizing me. I hold his gaze with outer calm.

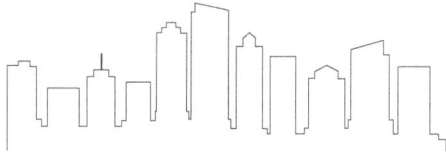

Chapter Seven

Sean takes a deep breath as he sits forward in his chair.

"Both Connor and Avery have support at their work sites so they will be able to clear their schedules to be with you most days.

"Unfortunately, my work has less flexibility; but will try to be here most evenings. Several of my builds are at a critical stage needing my close supervision."

"That is ok Sean. I know you will make time for me."

Connor tells us he will check in with Jake to confirm the meeting tonight still works for him and his team, he steps away to make the call.

Connor re-enters the room, verifying Jake will be here at six pm.

He scans the room ensuring he has our attention.

"The parole hearing will be held at the prison. There will be three members of the Parole Board that will make the decision regarding Price's parole.

"I submitted the Request to Observe on your behalf Allory, and they will review your Victim Statement at the hearing as well as prison personnel reports of how Price no longer poses a risk to society; therefore, able to serve the rest of his sentencing in the community.

"After the Board has reviewed all the information, they will decide whether to grant Price early parole.

"Any questions?" We all shake our heads.

Connor nods with approval, then he pivots.

"Jake will share with us his investigation into Price's illegal activities.

"He will detail what he knows about Price's associates' recent activities. He will touch on Interpol's role in the investigation of trafficking in Vancouver," concludes Connor.

Getting up from my seat, I sidle over to Sean. "I think the family chef would love to honour us with an excellent home-cooked meal."

Sean hops out of his chair, I follow along with him to the kitchen, Connor and Avery trailing behind us.

Sitting on stools in the kitchen, we keep Sean company as he prepares dinner. He efficiently readies the steaks to grill, makes chips in the oven then gathers salad fixing together.

Going into the fridge I bring out a bottle of wine for us girls and two beers for the guys.

Connor leans on the counter taking a sip of his beer. "How are things at the Museum, Allory?"

"I'm helping to develop the new exhibit; I'll contribute to remotely. There may be meetings to explore a partnership with UBC. It will help me focus on something positive while I am here."

Sipping our drinks, a quiet settles over the room aside from Sean chopping the salad.

Thoughts of facing Price tomorrow, causes a cascade of emotions inside me. Fear, anger, grief. I slam a figurative wall around my emotions. I can't afford to fall apart before or during the hearing.

It will take all my strength and fortitude to face him tomorrow.

I'm glad my family can't hear my thoughts.

Sean is just plating marinated steaks from the grill, then takes the fries out of the oven putting them into a warmed basket that he brings to the counter. He grabs the salad and dressing from the fridge.

We are mostly quiet eating our meals. Sean is truly the best cook, and the food is delicious.

Sean updates us about his new building projects. "My company is so busy that we hired another foreman."

Avery comes clean about her workload.

"My staff will do most of the work to allow me to spend time with Allory.

"There is a new client who wants me to do a major renovation in her home. Our first meeting in person is set for Tuesday afternoon in Aldergrove. After that my time will be spent with Allory."

"In the evenings we can play crib or Liar's dice," interrupts Sean.

"I'm glad you are a good loser as defeat awaits you."

"Don't be too sure of yourself, baby sister," he taunts me. "I plan to stay for a while after the meeting tonight. Let the games begin!"

"I accept your challenge," I threaten playfully.

Interrupting with a benevolent smile, Avery tells us she anticipated we would want to play. "The crib board, deck of cards, cups and dice are in the cupboard in the living room."

I think back to how competitive we are with games. I often won at cards but seldom won at dice. It was just the two of us, since Connor and Avery always declined to play with us. They said there was too much fierce competition between the two of us for their taste.

When we finish our after- dinner coffees, Avery and I tidy the kitchen.

We join our brothers in the living room. Sean pulls the cream-coloured drapes as dusk darkens the sky. Connor turns on the gas fireplace to provide heat. No sounds of traffic intrude from the street.

The elevator dings in the hallway, Jake arriving right on the dot of six pm.

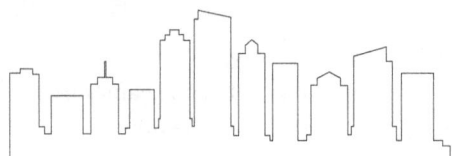

Chapter Eight

Jake has known my family well before he started protecting me when I left for France.

"Hi gang, we have an hour before Angel and Marc arrive to catch up on a few details." He sits down in the one available chair next to Connor.

"How was your flight Allory?"

"It was fine. I am not used to the rainy weather here, as it was balmy when I left Marseille. Good to see you, Jake."

"I prefer to take some time before the others arrive to go over a few plans I have been making for your protection Allory.

"We can assume that Price will have his associates following you closely when he becomes aware you are here.

"Angel will do nightly digital surveillance to identify any of Price's associates that come and go from around the condo. You will meet her shortly.

"Marc will provide part of the protection on outings with you Allory. In addition, two-man teams scouting outside places to identify risk and Price's associates following you. I can bring in extra security when needed.

"Until Price is released, I want you to be seen out and about with family and friends, Allory."

"Who is Marc," I ask.

"He is a close friend of mine who works for Interpol. He has been investigating human trafficking cases across international borders.

"Interpol has offered Marc's team to help in our investigation into Price's trafficking activities in Vancouver.

"Two years ago, I was approached by local policing to support them in their investigations into trafficking. The timing couldn't have been more perfect due to the alarming increase of trafficking in Vancouver.

"We modelled our team partnerships on successful private, public organizations working together to reduce trafficking in the U.S.

"With a nod from local policing, Marc and my team are taking the lead in the investigation into trafficking in Vancouver including transport of women and children to Asia and other jurisdictions.

"Allory, I recommend you spent time with Angel to get acquainted. She will provide support if there are any breaches of the building to get to you."

Jake fields a few more random questions from my brothers.

At seven o'clock the lobby security calls to say that we have visitors.

A man and a woman arrive in the elevator. Connor escorts them into the living room. Sean goes to get two more chairs for them to sit down with us.

Jake introduces Marc Lasalle and Angel Garcia.

Marc is a tall lean man with blonde hair and green eyes.

In comparison, Jake is shorter and broader with short black hair and blue eyes, his straightforward manner, always settles my jumpy nerves.

Angel is a slightly shorter woman of Asian descent with long dark hair. She smiles at me when Jake introduces her.

Connor provides introductions for himself, Sean, Avery, and me.

Marc greets my siblings; shaking their hands before his gaze turns to me.

"Hello Allory, pleased to meet you." He holds my hand for a moment in his before he takes a seat next to Jake.

"Marc, can you explain the role of Interpol and why you are in Vancouver," asks Jake.

"We often provide member nations' investigation resources they likely don't have or work with seconded police officers in the home country that integrate into a team.

"In this case, Interpol seconded RCMP making up most of my team. We are focused on tying Price directly to the trafficking in Vancouver.

"We currently suspect Price is guiding his men from prison. His men abduct local women and children holding them in a designated warehouse close to the docks until they are sold at an auction to foreign buyers. His men have access to the docks and a container to ship the women and children to Asia.

"Now we must unravel the links to prove Price, and his associates are selling woman and children right under the Port Authority's nose."

Marc's dark green gaze lingers on me for a moment, not enough to make me uncomfortable but I feel a blush rise on my cheeks.

Breaking eye contact with Marc, I study Jake's colleague Angel. She sits quietly next to Jake scanning the room.

Jake cedes the floor to Angel.

"The elevator to the condo will be locked down each night and downstairs security will scrutinize every person before they are allowed access to the condo. I have already given the names of your family and our teams to the security team downstairs. Tomorrow I will be updating them daily who will come and go to provide security for you."

I have a moment to realize this is really happening.

Tomorrow is the parole hearing.

I question, can I do this? Will I be able to see Price again without losing control?

The meeting winds down with Jake, Marc, and Angel.

Angel is setting up her computers for nighttime surveillance at the kitchen table.

Jake goes over the logistics for the parole hearing tomorrow.

"I will pick up Sean first around eight am. Connor and Allory by eight-thirty depending on traffic. That will leave us with enough time to drive out to the valley for the eleven o'clock parole hearing.

"See you all tomorrow morning." Jake leaves with Marc.

Before Avery leaves, I ask her to text me when she gets home from her meeting in the Valley tomorrow. I need to know she is safe.

Now it's Connor, Sean, Angel. And me.

"I need to make some calls and get some work done on my laptop. I will see you all in the morning," Connor says heading to one of bedrooms down the hall.

"Game on," grins Sean. He pulls out the crib board then cuts the cards.

We play for almost an hour. It's like old times. Yawning Sean concedes defeat.

"See you in the morning," he says gruffly as he kisses me on the cheek and gives me a final tight hug.

"I look forward to whipping your butt, tomorrow night," he says with a laugh as I walk with him to the elevator.

"See you in the morning," I tell him.

"We have this Al," he reassures me before the elevator door closes.

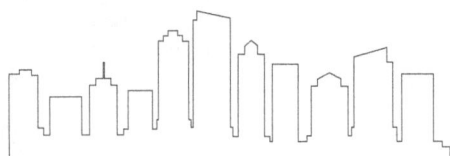

Chapter Nine

Connor comes out of the last bedroom at the base of the stairs just after Sean has left.

"Everyone else gone aside from Angel?"

"Yes, it is just you, and me."

Connor explains he has one final brief to review before tomorrow so he can send it off to his clerk. "Then I can focus all my attention on you and the parole hearing tomorrow."

"Okay.

"Try not to stay up too late. You look tired Connor."

"We will both benefit from a good night's sleep. See you in the morning."

"Allory," Angel asks, "can you bring down your phone and laptop? I need to add extra protection to your devices to prevent hacking."

Going upstairs, I return with my devices.

I visit awhile with her. She tells me about her girls and her Mum.

Yawning, "I confess, I'm still jetlagged." I wish her an uneventful night and head upstairs to bed.

"So, the initial meeting went well," Jake pauses.

Connor hears a door closing before Jake comes back on the phone.

"Yes, I think it went well but I want to talk about the part of the plan we won't be discussing with the rest of the group, the part where Allory will never be safe if we can't return Price to jail," says Connor quietly.

"Here is the plan," Jake begins. "There are two 'associates' I could get into the casual work pool in the Sherriff department. They would plan to be part of the transport after Price is charged.

"They have a history with Price and can handle what we are potentially asking if we can get them asylum in a warm country."

"This has to stay just between us Jake as I am not sure what my siblings or the rest of your team would say or do if they know what we are tentatively planning,"

"I agree but you are not the only one who thought this plan would be needed as back up," says Jake grimly.

"Thanks man, I hate to ask you to be involved with this Jake, but I don't see any other alternative."

"No need to worry Connor. We both know Price needs a permanent solution.

"On another note, I think the addition of Marc to the security protection will work well. I have known him for years and we have always had each other's backs".

"Good. Let's talk more tomorrow. I need some sleep if I am going to function. Thanks again Jake!"

After the two men hang up, Connor thinks about the conversation he just had with Jake. On an ethical level, the thought of removing Price permanently makes him feel like a monster. But in this case, we may need to be monsters to end this monster.

Connor refocuses his attention on the brief that is needed tomorrow. Once it's complete, he emails it to his clerk and closes the computer.

He is dogged tired. His shoulders feel heavy, like the weight of world is on them. Allory's safety preoccupies his thoughts. He can't bear the thought of failing her a second time.

After a quick shower, Connor leaves his door ajar before he crawls into bed, but sleep is elusive. Would all their planning be enough??

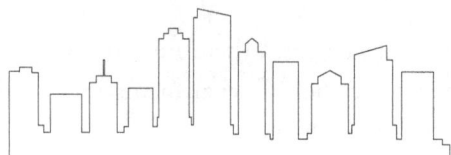

Chapter Ten

After saying goodnight to Angel, I get ready for bed then slide between the covers.

I close my eyes, and sleep comes quickly. Jarringly, I am pulled into one of my recurring nightmares.

It is that night, after a friend's party. I am the designated driver so after dropping off the last friend at home I decide not to go back to Gage Towers. My parents' house is closer.

Getting home, I take the back entrance to my room because my parents are having a party. I can hear the soft music and muted conversation as I climb the stairs to my third-floor bedroom. I lock the door once I am inside my room.

Removing my party dress, I drape it over the chair next to my bed. I'm thinking about how to celebrate my twenty-second birthday in a few days. I go to the bathroom to wash off my make-up and brush my teeth.

I am tired, needing a good sleep before early synchro practice in the morning. I turn out the lights and climb into bed. I fall asleep almost immediately.

Half wake, I sense something is not right. I start to reach for the bedside light although there is some light coming from the outside as I never close my drapes. I hear the door opening and conversation floating quietly up from downstairs. Then silence, awash in panic, sluggish from sleep. A tall figure stands over my bed. I recognize the person immediately. Before I can scream, he is on top of me, covering my mouth.

"Don't make a sound," he whispers "If you do, I will kill you. We are just going to have a bit of fun together."

He rips off the bed covers and straddles me at the waist. Shocking me, he tears the front of my pyjama top buttons spilling on the bed and floor. He pulls tape and his tie from his pocket. He grabs my wrists securing them with his tie and tape over my mouth to prevent me screaming.

With a violent rip he tears off my pyjama bottoms and tosses them to the floor.

"The things I have wanted to do to you," he whispers harshly in my ear.

"You have flaunted that beautiful body in front of me forever. Now I will do all the things I have been thinking about. You will tell no one about this or I will come back and kill you," he threatens again.

Struggling, he slaps me so hard my head aches. I try to get him off me while he restrains me. He rips off the tape on my mouth to kiss me. I bite him. He hits me so hard I lose awareness for a few moments.

When I rouse, he grabs my breasts clutching painfully while twisting my nipples until I have tears running down my cheeks. I notice the more I struggle, the more violent and aroused he gets in a way that frightens me.

He forces his penis down my throat. I gag and cannot breathe. He comes down my throat, I gasp for air. When he pulls out, he whispers dirty things into my ear. I almost throw up while he touches me everywhere including between my legs.

I have only been with one boy before tonight. The pain of his repeated penetration feels like he is ripping me apart. It goes on so long I go to a distant place in my head.

Until he flips me over on my stomach and penetrates my backside. I am beyond pain and reckoning. Before I lose consciousness, he leans down next to my ear.

"Tell no one. I would hate to come back and kill you. You are a sweet piece of ass. I will have you again," he whispers next to my ear.

I feel his weight lift off me and hear the bedroom door closing softly before I lose myself.

Not knowing how long I drifted in a sea of pain. Opening my eyes, panicked, as I look around my bedroom, liquid trickling down the inside of my legs. My phone is on the bedside table. I call Avery.

The details are fuzzy after that.

As the nightmare fades, bringing me back to the present. I remember Avery eventually telling me the story of how she got me to the hospital and through the sexual assault assessment, collection of evidence including DNA testing.

Still within in the edges of my nightmare, suddenly there is light. Connor is at my bedside. I crawl back against the headboard in fear. Connor's face is white as he looks at me cowering away from him like an animal.

"Take a deep breath, love. You are not in that room. You are here with me. Come back to me Allory."

With effort, I stop gasping for breath and focus on Connor's voice.

"I am here Al just take my hand. You are safe. No one can get to you now."

Connor sits on the floor next to the bed, while I hold his hand tightly, fighting to keep the nightmare away.

"Heard you cry out from downstairs; I left my bedroom door open."

I look to see my bedroom door ajar. I have the random thought that I never close my door ever since Price invaded my bedroom at home. I need to see anything coming at me.

Grimacing, "I am so sorry I woke you. I guess with everything tonight the nightmare just grabbed me."

Connor shakes his head. "You have nothing to be sorry about Al.

"We will do everything we can to ensure he goes back to prison again, this time permanently!"

I see tears in his eyes.

"I haven't had that dream in a long while. I guess it is being back in Vancouver and having to see Price at the parole hearing tomorrow. I am still committed to the plan."

"Allory, it's so hard to be putting you at risk again. But none of us are being naïve. Price will never stop unless we stop him. I just wish this was not going to be so hard on you," he says quietly as he kisses my forehead.

"Do you think you might go back to sleep? I can stay longer if you want me to," He climbs to his feet from the floor.

"No, I am good Connor. I will see you in the morning. Thank you!"

Leaving my door open, he goes back to his room.

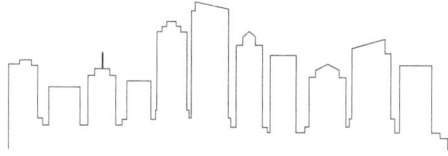

Chapter Eleven
Day Two Tuesday Am-Parole Hearing

Surprisingly, the nightmare doesn't return. I sleep the rest of the night and wake feeling rested.

Price had always been around even before the rape and abduction. He did business with my family. He always struck me as arrogant, and I could see the darkness in him.

I believe Price continues to have money and connections that make him overconfident. We will use that against him. In four days, we will see whether Leon Price comes for me right away or waits until my guard is down.

I shower, dress and join Connor for breakfast. He cooks my favourite blueberry pancakes.

Angel gives me back my phone and laptop prior to us leaving. She will go home to sleep and return this afternoon. It feels odd not being alone for a moment.

Avery texts, letting me know she is thinking about me today and will see me in early evening after her meeting.

The lobby calls telling us our ride is downstairs. Connor, and I exit to the street level. Jake is in the driver seat while Sean relocates from the front passenger's seat to climb in the back with Connor and me.

The prison is an hour drive outside the city. I hardly pay attention to the green pastoral views from the freeway as we leave the city. Connor and Sean sit quietly, occasionally checking their cell phones.

I declined to read my victim statement today. My purpose to attend the hearing is to remind him I am back in Vancouver. Feeling vulnerable and anxious is a nasty combination when I must put on a brave face at the parole hearing.

I knew from his sexual assault trial and sentencing that Price would do everything to secure an early parole. The only positive I can see coming out of today is he will be branded a rapist as part of the national sex offender registry managed by the RCMP.

Perhaps it will be harder for him to target me then? Still, I am sure, he will come for me once he is released.

The rains from yesterday have changed to blue sky with hazy clouds near the mountains. I can't appreciate the view due to the churning pit of fear in my stomach and the shiver of cold sweat.

"Hey Jake, can you turn up the heat in the back?" Sean asks without looking at me.

"Sure, man. Let me know if you get too hot." Jake flicks a look at us in rear-view mirror before looking back to the road., I can't verify if he realizes I am almost losing it in the backseat.

Connor grabs a light blanket that was hanging over his side of the seat and drapes it over my shoulders. I give him a grateful look. I know I will lose my composure if I say anything. He squeezes my shoulder and returns to his phone messages.

Getting to the prison, I question my readiness to see the man who created all my nightmares. Jake opens my door as my brothers get out the other side at the gate house.

We are met by a guard. Connor deals with the sign in, and visitor passes. We are directed to a low-lying building on the left where the Parole Board hearing will take place.

Connor leads the way through the glass doors and down a corridor lined by cream-coloured walls and tiled floors. Our steps, loud echoes in the empty hall. A row of chairs is at the end of the corridor next to a wooden door.

"This is where we are to sit until the clerk comes to get us," says Connor quietly. My brothers sit down on either side of me.

"Al are you okay?" whispers Sean.

"No" I grimace, "but thanks for asking."

Sean slips a warm hand through mine that is icy cold.

Worry on his face, Connor peers at me but doesn't say anything.

A clerk comes to direct us to the hearing room lacking natural lightening. The three Parole Board members sit to the right side.

We are directed to chairs in the back of the room.

In the front of the Board sits Price and his lawyer with their backs to us. I remember the lawyer from Price's trial as they both turn around when me and my brothers enter the room. Price tries to make eye contact with me for several long minutes before facing the Parole Board again. Sean grabs my hand tightly as I start to shake.

I almost don't hear the Parole Board member to the far-left start speaking.

"The Board will review in detail the Victim Statement, what team leaders; prison guards and counselors have to say about positive change and personal growth attained by Mr. Price while in this facility.

"Their opinions will be part of helping us determine if he is ready to safely integrate back into the community.

"Then Mr. Price will describe his efforts in prison to demonstrate remorse for his actions and explain why he no longer poses a risk to the community. If granted early parole, he will serve the remainder of his original sentence in the community."

As the chairman continues to explain the hearing process, I am suddenly furiously angry. This piece of crap is going to get out of prison while convincing everyone he has rehabilitated and is safe to live in the community. He has spent less than two years of his sentence on the inside. I look around at the Parole board and officers ready to explain how Price has repented for his sins. All lies. He is smart enough to fool everyone.

Connor leans over and whispers in my ear. "He may get out of here, but things are far from over. Don't let him see he is getting to you. We stand with you this time and always."

The hearing drags on for what seems forever. The room is airless.

My Victim Statement is read out loud. I am hopeful to see the Parole Board members frowning with the detail I included in the attack.

Listening to my testimonial of what Price did me, I wonder if I will ever stop feeling fearful, shameful, and angry because of what Price did to me?

In contrast the prison personnel including guards, counsellor and pastor present a positive impression of Price's rehabilitation. The hardest part is having to listen to Price be contrite. I knew he was lying through his teeth.

There is a brief recess while the Parole Board reviews the presented information. Then we are invited back to our seats in the hearing room.

I hear the unanimous decision to grant Price parole from a long dark tunnel. The conditions of release are carefully explained. Price will be released on Friday. That is only four days away, when he will complete his sentencing in the community. He will be registered in the national sexual offender's registry and must adhere to the rules laid out by the Board and restrictions therein.

As we stand to leave, Price looks over his shoulder directly at me. A wicked smirk on his face as his gaze peruses me from my head to my toes. Lingering on my breasts for a long moment.

He makes me feel dirty while my rage blazes, waiting to erupt.

Turning my back to Price, I tuck my hand through Connor's arm. He and Sean saw how Price looked at me. Taking a breath, I remember we plan to make this monster pay.

I can't wait to get outside and away from here. My brothers follow me to the outside gate. Connor returns our visitor passes to the gatekeeper, and we all walk over to the car.

Once inside, my brothers say nothing at first. I am still so angry I can barely speak. Being furious is better than paralyzed with fear in this moment.

Clamping down the fury for a moment, I turn toward Connor and Sean.

"I couldn't have done this without you both so thank you," I choke out.

Fine shivers wrack my body. I ask Jake, "Before we get to the freeway, can we stop on a side street where there are no houses?"

Jake pulls into an empty cul-de-sac a few minutes later. I open my door just as we are stopped. I jump out of the car and scream out my rage. Angry tears running down my face.

When Sean jumps out of the car, I hold my hands out to keep him away. I pound and kick the side of the car. That bastard is not remorseful or rehabilitated. Unleashing my fury feels cathartic.

Price will come for me again, but this time I won't be tipsy, drugged or alone. I may be scared spitless, but my anger fuels my recommitment to making Price pay for what he has done to me and other women.

Pulling me down next to him in the gravel, Sean drags me close. This brother, who has always walked beside me. He usually expresses his feelings loudly while Connor is quiet and controlled. Leaning next to me, he holds me close. We need no words between us. Just a quiet space before we return to the car.

Eventually, Sean helps me off the ground, and we all get back in the car.

"I can't tell you not to be afraid Al, but this time Connor, Avery and I will stand with you. Jake will keep you as safe as we can."

———

Leon Price calls Luis Diaz his second in command after the parole hearing from the inmate phone.

When Luis answers he begins giving him instructions before hanging up.

At two pm Leon is escorted by the prison guard to another dingy and depressing visiting area. He realizes that in four days' time he won't have to talk behind a partition.

Luis arrives smiling as he picks up the phone on his side of the partition while Leon is doing the same on his side.

"I assume you will be paroled on Friday?"

"Yes. I need you to arrange things for me before I am released.

"I want you to become acquainted with and stay close to the siblings. Arrange a few friendly encounters. I would like several of our teams to provide security for the youngest sister to protect her until I get released."

"I will get on that starting this afternoon," Luis promises

"I also want Art Gallery Gala tickets for Friday for me and two of our teams.

"Arrange to come back on Thursday to drop off my suit and underclothing I will wear on Friday when I am released from this pit."

His final directive, "Be here on Friday for nine am sharp to drive me back to the city."

"Ok, boss see you." He hands up the phone giving Price a salute as he leaves.

———

Chapter Twelve

Scanning out the window, we pass familiar neighbourhoods. I feel detached with numbness and shock that Price got parole even though I had known he would. There was a tiny part of me that hoped he would stay in jail so he couldn't continue to ruin my life.

Sean gets on his cell to order lunch to be delivered while Connor calls the condo concierge to expect a lunch delivery.

Feeling like I am floating, distant from my emotions after expelling all that rage, I didn't consciously know I had it in me.

Finally, we are back at the condo.

Sean smiles when the condo phone rings. "Lunch" he says walking to the elevator to receive the food.

Going to the bathroom to wash my hands, I delay the inevitable conversation about the parole hearing.

Sean has already brought the burgers and fries, plates and a jug of water to the table. Jake and Connor are already seated.

Jake is the first to break the silence.

"Now we flaunt you in his face around town to ensure he remains committed to coming after you once he is back in the community.

"We calculate his timeline for his next shipment of women and children will be sold and shipped to Asia as early as Saturday.

"Factoring in that Price's associates will follow you until Price gives the order to abduct you. I may be is underestimating, thinking he will try to keep you in reasonable shape to sell you at the auction and transport to the buyer in Asia. His brutality has been honed in prison so we should factor that in."

It appears that Jake and I are on the same wavelength about Price's future actions after he gets out of prison.

"We are going to use all our surveillance and security measures to keep you safe now including GPS technology," Jake explains.

"Our best option is a small GPS Tracker Button to enable us to locate and find you when you are away from the condo.

"The buttons are intended to blend into clothing. I will bring them to you tomorrow morning.

"One of my men has been shadowing Price's second in command for months now. If I had to make an educated guess, Price knew where you were all this time and even when your flight arrived at YVR."

Shivering, a cold chill runs down my back thinking how naïve I was feeling safe in France; and since I arrived in Vancouver. Price knew where I was the whole time.

Small consolation with Price getting parole, I will never be alone.

"Through the remainder of the week Marc will begin to take you places to establish him as your boyfriend from Marseille. He will begin to stay here with you in the condo," Jake explains

"Meanwhile my team and Marc's will find the warehouse and the manifests at the dock for the container and ship that will be bound for Asia with human cargo.

"I will continue to have a man on Price's second in command to see what other instructions Price gives him before he is paroled."

"Jake, I will be working remotely for the Museum. One of my tasks is to meet with UBC. I hope to have a first meeting scheduled with my work contact within the next two days.

"I contacted a few friends from university for lunch this week.

"Connor, I'm assuming you and Sean need to get back to work.

"My plan is to spend the afternoon dealing with emails and drafting preliminary ideas for my UBC meeting."

Allory walks with Connor to the bedroom where he left his overnight bag.

"Connor, I don't feel right about you all covering the cost of additional security and the condo. Will you at least let me contribute whatever amount I am comfortable with?"

"Avery, Sean, and I will cover the expenses. We see it as an investment in our family meaning you, me, Avery and Sean. It eases our minds to provide the security while we make Price pay for his crimes"

"I will find another way to thank you."

Connor grabs his overnight bag. He wraps an arm around me as I walk him to the exit.

"Time permitting, I may drop by after work to see how things are going."

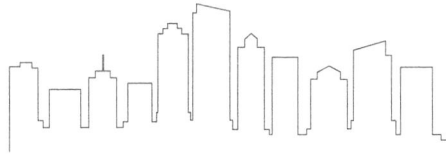

Chapter Thirteen

Now it's just us girls in the condo with Angel at the kitchen table monitoring surveillance.

The afternoon passes quickly as I work on my laptop next to her.

I have collated ideas for a presentation at UBC. I sent an email to my contact Aaron Summers to see if he and his team can meet with me Wednesday or Thursday preferably in the morning.

I spend the rest of the day planning when to connect with Andre and Céline with the nine-hour time difference between Vancouver and Marseille. I always find it confusing.

Sean arrives around six pm.

Connor drops by as he had a cancelled meeting and wanted to check that I was okay after the parole hearing.

I am checking for a text from Avery as she should be on her way home from her meeting in Aldergrove.

Connor and I listen to Sean describing the progress of his new builds.

It is now six forty-five, no text from Avery.

The elevator arrives with Jake and Marc. They go to talk with Angel at the kitchen table.

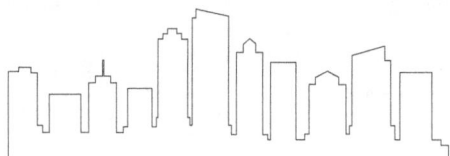

Chapter Fourteen
Tuesday morning

Avery has been up since seven am. She rubs her tired eyes that have been focusing on her computer for hours. She is feeling a bit anxious about the coming meeting this afternoon with a new client in Aldergrove.

Her initial phone consult with her new client was several weeks ago.

She has drafted initial ideas to present this afternoon.

Yesterday while Allory took her nap, she had a productive virtual meeting with her administrative assistant and intern. She was pleased with their work plans they developed and commended both for the excellent work they had been doing.

They didn't seem apprehensive that she would be out of the office for the next ten days. She reassured her staff they could connect with her by phone or email if something unexpected came up.

Checking the clock, satisfied she had time to eat lunch while watching the noon news on Global before showering and changing. Knowing she needed to be out in Aldergrove by four-thirty.

Taking the elevator to the parkade, she unlocks her car setting her briefcase in the backseat. She decides to avoid the heavier traffic heading north to Highway Ten and Aldergrove.

She is tense about this meeting, which is strange. Typically, she loves in person visits. Why she is worried about this meeting mystifies her.

The traffic going out of Vancouver is light and she reaches her destination on time. Turning into the driveway, she pulls up close to the house. She grabs her briefcase from the backseat and walks up to the front door as it opens.

"Hello Mrs. Andrews, pleased to meet you in person," Avery smiles and shakes her hand before she is led into the house.

Glancing around she sees a beautiful home with large windows and vaulted ceiling, décor in pleasing colours. Her client leads her into a tastefully decorated office.

"You have a lovely home," compliments Avery.

Her client sits down behind the desk gesturing for Avery to take a seat across from her.

She tells herself to ignore the formality and distance exhibited by her client, but her discomfort persists.

Pulling two copies of her initial ideas for the room renovation from her briefcase, she hands her client a copy to follow along as they talk.

They discuss Avery's draft ideas based on their initial phone consultation.

Avery requests to see the room that will be renovated to get a better handle on what the client wants as their initial discussion makes her realize that they may not be on the same page.

She walks with her client down the hallway, Mrs. Andrews opens the second door on the right. "This is my husband's study," she tells me.

"Please elaborate on your ideas for the room renovation."

I jot down notes, while encouraging her to further flesh out the vision she is looking for.

It is close to six o'clock when we wrap the meeting up.

"Avery, I request you send your drafted plans next week by email to me".

"Yes, that is doable Mrs. Andrews. The next steps will be to finalize the plan and discuss who will be contracted to do the renovation work."

We shake hands before she opens the front door. "I will be in touch with you in two weeks. It has been a pleasure meeting you." Avery descends the stairs to the drive.

She stows her briefcase on the front passenger seat, then backs out of the driveway. She is relieved to be driving home. Thinking how cold her client was to her. Realizing she needs to get over it because doing this renovation will be profitable for her company.

She is almost to the freeway exiting from Highway Ten when she sees a car gaining quickly behind her on a narrow stretch of the road. There is no room for the car to pass. The car accelerates, coming up to her bumper and rams it hard. She tries to stay on the road, but the car rams against her a second time forcing her to skid off the road into a deep ditch.

The car rolls over and Avery loses consciousness.

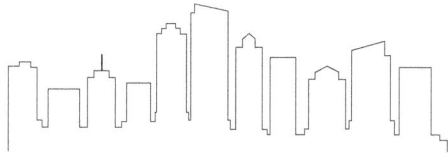

Chapter Fifteen
Tuesday Night

Checking the time, it is nearly seven o'clock. I don't have a text from my sister. What has happened to Avery?

Jake, Marc, Sean and Connor are discussing security.

"I hate to be an alarmist, but Avery hasn't texted me after her meeting in Aldergrove. You all know she is super diligent about checking in, I'm worried."

Jake sends Connor a disturbed look. "I will call the RCMP to see if there has been a traffic accident on that stretch of the highway."

Within ten minutes, Jake hangs up his phone.

"There was a single car accident around six-thirty pm on Highway Ten with first responders rescuing an injured female driver who was taken to White Rock Hospital."

Connor calls the hospital asking for the admission department. He asks if a patient Avery Landry has been admitted.

He hangs up. "She is still in emergency but will be admitted to the ward shortly."

Jake sees the panic on our faces. Picking up his phone he starts giving rapid instructions to someone at his office.

"Contact Lea, Ken, and Jase asking them to meet me at White Rock Hospital."

Ushering Allory, Sean and Connor into the arriving elevator, Jake pushes the button for the parkade.

Arriving at the hospital forty-five minutes later, they discover that Avery has been admitted upstairs to the ward for observation overnight.

Connor goes to talk with the nurse while Sean and I enter her room almost soundlessly.

Avery's eyes are closed. We can see her chest lifting with each breath.

Returning Connor stands next to Sean and me at the foot of Avery's bed.

"Avery's x-rays are negative for fractures which is a miracle after the crash. She has a concussion and multiple scrapes and bruising requiring observation overnight."

"I want to stay with her tonight, Connor. Could you arrange a private room for her?"

He leaves to talk with the nurse. When Connor returns, he tells us, "Fortunately, there is a vacant private room next door. The nurse will have the orderly help transfer Avery."

Lea arrives to provide security already being briefed by Jake about what happened to Avery.

Asking Sean and Allory to follow him, Connor leads them to a small waiting room down the hall to discuss his conversation with the RCMP officer who attended the scene of Avery's accident.

"Apparently, there was a witness to the accident who called the RCMP and stayed with Avery until the First Responders arrived. He was able to provide a description of the car make and model but unfortunately the license plates were scrubbed.

"Allory, I know you want to stay the night with Avery. I am confident that Lea will guard you both from harm. Sean and I will go home with Jake.

"Jake and I will return to pick you up when Avery is discharged in the morning."

We walk back to Avery's room, Jake, Connor and Sean peek in to see Avery sleeping with Lea standing in front of the window next to Avery's bed. They whisper good night before leaving.

I go into Avery's room and pull a chair close to the bed. I gently hold her hand as she sleeps.

It is a long night as I keep watch over my sister. I get up every few hours to stretch the kinks out. Lea is a quiet presence standing close to the door.

In the morning, the doctor arrives early to reassess Avery. He is satisfied that she can be discharged home with instructions to follow up with her family physician in a day or two. After he leaves, I go into the hallway to call Connor to pick us up.

Later in the morning Jake and Connor arrive. Lea leaves the room to give us privacy to talk while she hunts down a wheelchair to get Avery to the car.

Avery is more aware and awake then she was last night. It is obvious she is in pain when she moves in bed, needing help to sit up on propped pillows behind her back.

Jake catches Avery's gaze. "Connor and I think it is best you stay at the condo with Allory to ensure you both have added protection."

Avery nods her agreement of the plan. A nurse comes in to give her pain medication to help her manage on the drive back to the condo.

The nurse gives a pain prescription to me.

I go downstairs with Lea to the pharmacy to fill the prescription before we leave.

Once in the car Avery leans against my shoulder and dozes for the whole trip back.

Chapter Sixteen
Wed morning Day three

When we arrive at the condo parkade, Connor helps Avery out of the car taking her in his arms, he carries her into the elevator and then upstairs to the enjoining bedroom next to mine.

I help her remove her clothes, assisting her into a nighty. I settle her into bed, leaving her bedroom door open so I could hear if she needs me. She is fast asleep before I leave the room.

I plan to get some sleep myself but wanted to check with everyone downstairs first.

When I get downstairs Jake, Connor, Sean, Marc, Angel and Lea are at the dining room table debriefing about last night.

I sit down next to Angel. "I went home to sleep last night as Leo took over surveillance from the office. I will be here all day while Lea goes home to sleep," she explains quietly under the guy's voices.

There is a lull in their conversation, I grab Connor's sleeve to catch his attention.

"Did you have Avery's car towed to the garage and retrieved her briefcase. When she is more coherent that will be her first concern."

"Her car is totalled but I ran by the wrecking yard to get her briefcase. There were no other things salvageable. I have started an ICBC claim on her behalf."

"Jake, having a lot of free time at the hospital, I texted Aaron Summers to cancel our meeting for this morning. Fortunately, he was able to juggle his team's schedule to have the meeting on Thursday at eleven-thirty am.

"I called Avery's doctor's office; she has an appointment for nine-thirty tomorrow morning.

I also connected with my UBC friends who can meet either Thursday or Friday for lunch."

"That sounds fine Allory," Jake reassures me.

"I am bushed from the long night. I will see you all later after I get some sleep."

I check on Avery, she is sleeping. I leave her door wide open to hear her if she wakes.

Lying in bed, I'm exhausted but sleep eludes me. I shiver at the thought of Avery's accident. She could have been seriously injured or killed. All because Price has a vendetta against me and now my family.

Guilt plagues me that my sister was injured because of me. Even though, when she wakes, I know she will be adamant about continuing to support me, despite being targeted by a Price associate.

I'm sick of being afraid. That look from Price at the parole hearing secretly terrified me. Yet at the same time it impels me to not give in or abandon our pursuit to have him incarcerated for life.

Yet, as the sacrificial lamb this time, I am not confident that I will escape as easily as I did the last time.

Despite utilizing deep breathing and mindfulness to shut down intrusive thoughts, it takes longer than normal to succumb to sleep.

Waking just after four pm. My thoughts running in circles, my dreams, elusive shadows. I check on Avery who is thankfully still asleep.

I change from my pyjamas into my swimsuit and gather my other gear heading downstairs.

My brothers look tense as they talk with Jake and Marc in the living room. Angel is at the kitchen table with her computers.

Jake looks up, noticing my swimming gear. Picking up the phone he arranges closure of the pool and a security guard at the door.

"Two hours max then you come back here," Jake orders. Marc stands up and follows me to the elevator.

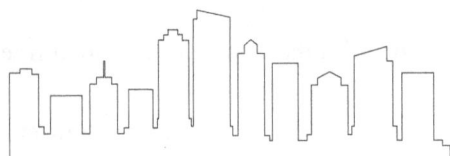

Chapter Seventeen
Wed pm

Marc and I get into the elevator descending to the fourth floor. When the elevator door opens, silently we walk down the hall to the pool entrance where security is waiting at the door to let us in.

Marc sits in a recliner at the edge of the pool deck, a silent presence yet not intrusive. Dropping my robe and towel, I don my swimming goggles and cap before diving into the pool slicing through the water with ease.

I swim lengths starting with freestyle, then back stroke followed by butterfly. I also spend time in the deep end practicing synchro until I start to lag.

Gripping the edge of the pool, I lift myself onto the pool deck feeling less suffocated by the recent events with Avery. The fear washed away for now. Towelling dry, I wrap myself in my robe, sliding on my flip flops.

I thank the security guard on our way out, retaking the elevator upstairs with Marc who remains a quiet presence next to me.

My brothers are still here. Jake is in the living room talking on his cell. He ends his call when Marc and I come into the room.

"Thanks to both of you for the swim, I really needed the exercise because it calms me down." I leave Marc and Jake with my brothers.

I go upstairs to shower and change.

I check on Avery who is still sleeping. I am not surprised as she was restless in the hospital last night with little restorative sleep.

When I return downstairs Jake, Sean and Connor were gone.

"Angel, where did the guys go?"

"Sean got a call from his foreman at one of his worksites when you went upstairs.

"Connor couldn't stay either as he had to meet with an important client before the end of the business day."

"What should I order in for dinner?" asking as I plunk down in the chair next to Angel.

"Jake and Marc would likely go for burgers after their virtual meeting with Marc's team. A salad would be good as I am eating a later dinner with my girls after their soccer practice."

I get on my phone to order burgers and four small salads to be delivered.

I go upstairs to wake Avery. She is slow to open her eyes and groans in pain when she turns in bed to look at me.

I help her out of bed into the bathroom. I sit her on the edge of the tub while I get two pain pills and a glass of water to wash them down.

I leave her to use the toilet and come in after she has washed her hands and brushed her teeth.

I help her into a robe then walk beside her into the bedroom. She sits on the bed, while I help her lift her legs on to the mattress while she leans back against the propped-up pillows.

Avery has pinched look on her face with the scrapes and bruises more apparent than last night.

"Would you like something to eat and drink?"

She perks up with the thought of food. "I would love a cup of tea and maybe peanut butter toast after the pain medicine kicks in."

Avery closes her eyes exhausted from getting up to the bathroom.

I sit in the chair across from the bed checking my emails and texts on my phone. I re-read the texts from my friends. They are so excited to meet on Thursday for lunch.

I send a text to Céline asking if she has time to talk tonight at ten-thirty Vancouver time which will be before she goes to work.

Going down to the kitchen I make Avery's toast and tea and bring it up to the bedroom. I wake her helping her to sit up against the pillows. I put the tray with toast and tea on her lap. She eats and drinks slowly

Once she is finished, I remove the tray and set it by the door.

"Avery, would you like a bath?" I ask.

"Yes" she replies. I feel so grungy!

"I will be tuckered out by the exertion, but I want to be clean! Soaking my aches and pains sounds heavenly."

After running the bath, I set a small towel on the edge of tub where I help her sit after removing her nighty. She shifts as I lift one leg then the other into the tub. I help her shift her weight to lower herself into the water. I hand her the washcloth and give her privacy to bathe.

Sitting reading an e-book until I hear Avery calling me to help her out of the tub. I sit her on the tub edge to dry her off with a large bath towel. I am shocked to see her bruising has spread over her entire torso; her arms and legs covered in scrapes.

I help her into a clean nightie and walk her into her bedroom, I had already turned the covers down and positioned her pillows for maximum comfort while she sleeps. She sits down gingerly on the bed as I gently swing her legs onto the mattress while she groans, lying back against the pillows.

"I feel like a little old lady," she gasps once settled in bed.

I hold Avery's hand until she falls asleep. I take the food tray and teapot down to the kitchen.

I see Angel and Lea at the kitchen table. Angel interrupts her conversation.

"Jake took his burger and left for his office. While Marc ate his burger before trying to arrange a call with his superior in Lyon. The salads are great you should have one with your burger."

I eat my dinner and tidy up the kitchen before I go upstairs likely having an early night. I can't wait for Avery to see her doctor tomorrow to ensure there is nothing else we can do to help her heal.

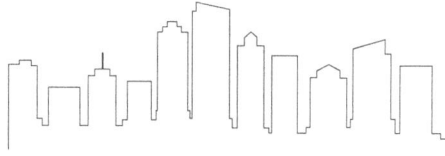

Chapter Eighteen
Day Thurs am*

I think I drifted off quickly last night.

Since Monday's flight, the parole hearing and Avery's car accident Tuesday I realize my body just shut down for a while.

I hear Avery in the bathroom so can count on she will not want to stay in bed all day.

Avery's a doctor appointment is at nine-thirty am.

Marc and I need to be at UBC for eleven-thirty am.

Avery comes out of the bathroom showered and dressed. She is moving better than yesterday but I worry that she will overdo it.

"Rest, Avery while I shower and dress."

"That sounds good, the shower tired me out. I have little old lady syndrome again," she jokes.

I shower and dress in record time and go downstairs with Avery, ensuring she sits in a comfortable chair in the living room while I make breakfast.

I find Lea and Angel at the kitchen table.

Avery comes to ask Lea if she could take her home after her doctor appointment to get some of her things from her condo to bring here. Lea agrees to discuss it when Jake arrives.

Settling at the dining table, Avery waits for me to bring breakfast in.

"If you are feeling better tomorrow you can go to lunch with me and Marc to meet some of my friends."

"I am not sure about lunch. I want to see how I do after the doctor appointment. And if Jake okays me going home for a while."

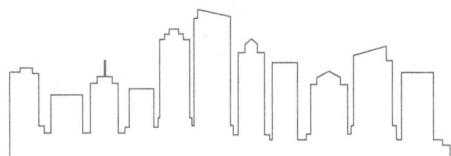

Chapter Nineteen
Thurs am

Jake, Marc, and Connor arrive together.

Jake, Marc and Angel settle around the kitchen table room table where Lea has left her laptops. Jake has brought additional electronics devices he sets down on the table.

Connor leads his sisters into the living room to have a private conversation with them.

Connor looks so serious.

"I have bad news to tell you girls about me and Sean.

"I had a near miss accident yesterday afternoon while waiting for a traffic light to cross Burrard Street. Someone pushed me so hard I was shoved into the oncoming traffic. Fortunately, before I was run over Ken was able to yank me back on to the sidewalk.

"There was no witness that saw the person who pushed me. The incident was reported to the police. It was fortunate that Ken took quick action to pull me back onto the sidewalk.

"To add to our problems Sean had a suspicious fire at one of his's work-sites late yesterday. Fortunately, the fire was caught early, one worker with a minor burn. It unfortunately caused substantial damage to the building and setting the projected finish date back.

"The fire marshal and WorkSafe are investigating. Right now, Sean is overwhelmed, staying ahead of the situation, so he asked me to tell you both what happened. He hopes to stop by tonight."

Avery and I are pale and shaking when Connor is finished telling us the bad news.

"Girls, both Sean and I are okay and handling the situations."

"Connor, I feel this is all my fault," cries Allory.

"Allory, this is an attempt to scare you by targeting us. We are stronger together. You need to remember that."

Connor goes to get Jake, Marc, and Angel to plan for today's outings.

Allory outlines her plans.

"I want to go with Avery to her appointment at nine-thirty.

"Then Marc and I have my presentation at UBC for eleven-thirty."

Jake steps away to call his office to confirm security for Avery's doctor appointment and UBC meeting. He returns, giving us a thumbs up.

Connor describes the parole restrictions placed on Price once he is released on Friday.

"He will be restricted to his residence and workplace. He is unable to leave the country. He is to refrain from associations with people involved in criminal activities. Other special restrictions of his release are to avoid drugs and alcohol. He is to have no contact with Allory."

Allory is dubious that Price will adhere to the restrictions. "It won't stop him; he will just figure out how to bend them."

"Jake, Can Lea take me home this morning after my doctor appointment to get some of my things to bring back here?"

"I'm okay with that plan Avery, but I am adding Troy to your security detail to ensure Lea gets enough rest.

"Angel has a personal matter to attend to. Leo will cover surveillance around the condo from the office until Angel returns."

"Jake, I am flexible about outings for the next few days.

"It will be nice to not have to worry about bumping into Price before Friday. I know he will have his associates follow me, but I trust you to have that covered.

"This morning, I texted my UBC friends again. They are open for lunch tomorrow at noon on the Westside."

"These sound like viable ideas for the next few days," says Jake.

Giving Allory the two GPS buttons, Jake explains "Allory please wear one on your shirt and put the other in your purse when away from condo to enable Leo to keep track of your location."

"Allory, it might be helpful if you explain your remote work," suggests Connor.

He notes with pride that Allory comes alive when she talks about her work and love for history.

"Typically, I will work remotely in the mornings on the new exhibit that will open in a few months at the Marseille Museum. I will also have in-person meetings at UBC to explore a partnership between the university and my museum starting today."

"Allory can you confirm with Aaron Sumner the meeting this morning," requests Jake.

I step away to call my UBC contact.

"Hi Aaron, I just want to check that the meeting at eleven-thirty is still on and that you are okay with me bringing a colleague?"

"Yes, Allory that will fine. I look forward to meeting you both."

I re-enter the room. "It is a go for UBC for eleven-thirty. It is now nine-thirty. I already have prepared a short presentation for the meeting today. If we leave by ten-fifty we should arrive on time."

"An outing for Marc and Allory to Stanley Park Tea House this afternoon is a good option," Connor suggests.

"It should be easy to make a reservation and ensure security, right Jake?"

"I will ask Leo to make a reservation for three pm and send a detail to scout the premises."

Allory, Lea and Avery leave to go her doctor appointment. Meeting Troy in the parkade.

"Jake will that leave you enough time to get security in place for Stanley Park today?" Connor asks.

"Yes, it is doable," Jake says. "I sent a team out to UBC earlier to investigate possible dangers at the building where Allory will attend the meeting. After the UBC meeting the team will check out any security issues at the Teahouse.

"I will drive them to and from UBC and the Teahouse.

"I just got a text from Leo confirming all the arrangements for this afternoon. He sent the Teahouse reservation to your phone Marc."

"Ok as usual you have everything under control," praises Connor. "I have a meeting with a client at my office at nine-thirty. I will check in with you later in the day."

Jake looks at his watch. "Marc it is almost nine o'clock. I need to check in at the office. I'm hoping you can stay with Allory when she returns to the condo until it's time to go to UBC.

"When I get back you can go get your stuff at the hotel and leave it in a spare room here. Will that work for you?"

I shrug, "No problem, Jake. I'll check in with my team to see what progress they have made identifying the warehouse and the manifests at the docks. I have a call with the Port Authority CFO in about ten minutes."

Lea, Avery and Allory arrive shortly after Marc finishes with his call.

"I need to grab my laptop that Connor retrieved from my car and a few things I want to leave at home," Avery calls over her shoulder heading upstairs.

While Avery is gathering her things Allory takes the opportunity to change into a cream blouse, black pencil skirt, stockings and shoes. She takes a red blazer from the closet she will wear overtop when they leave for the UBC meeting.

"Have a good rest at home Avery," I say watching her and Lea leave.

I put one of the GPS trackers on the lapel of my red blazer. The second one in my purse zipped into an inside pocket of my briefcase next to my laptop.

I sit down at the living room table across from Marc. "I don't need to check my UBC presentation as I reviewed it last night before bed."

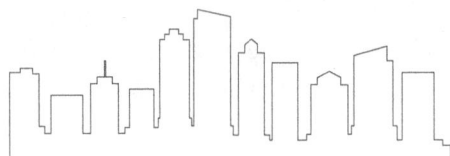

Chapter Twenty
Tues later morning

Now I am with I guy who I don't know. And I am nervous.

"Allory, I know this is hard, but we need to take the time to get to know each other better, it will help us when we go on outings."

"I will go first. Can we converse in French?"

"Merci Marc, D'accord."

"I am thirty-one years old. I have a house in Provence a short distance from my family home and keep an apartment in Marseille for work purposes. My parents own a winery. I went to school in Paris graduating with a degree in history."

He has a faraway look in his eyes for a few seconds before he regains his composure.

"I had plans to continue with graduate studies until my sister was abducted while on holiday by human traffickers the summer before school restarted. She was never found and as you can imagine it was devastating for me and my family."

Allory is silenced for a moment. Horrified that both Marc and her have been shattered by the evil of traffickers.

After a few moments I realize words are not enough. I lean over and clasp Marc's hand. When I go to release him, he takes my hand enfolding it with his, continuing our conversation.

"I met Jake when we were at university in Paris.

"Jake's mother's family is French. He convinced me to join the French Army as impetus to deal with the loss of my sister.

"I left after three years to join Interpol working with teams assigned to trafficking.

"I travel a lot in my job because Interpol works with many nation members."

"Marc, I'm so sorry to hear about your sister. I don't really know what to say.

"I can see why you and Jake are willing to help us."

He nods, dark shadows in his eyes as he shares his grief. We sit for several minutes allowing Marc to collect himself.

"My studies at UBC were focused on history but I did take a few courses in health sciences to see if I wanted to go in that direction. History turned out to be where my passions lay. I joined the UBC synchronized swimming team for fun but found I liked the competitiveness of the sport.

"I'm the baby of the family. Connor is seven years older than me; Avery five, and Sean three. I was an oops baby and spent most of my early years chasing after my siblings.

"At the time of the rape and abduction; I'd completed my degree with honors. I'd applied at Paris University for a two-year Master's History program. My plan was to move right after the graduation ceremony if I was accepted.

"Leaving Vancouver for Paris the week after I received my letter, was a relief yet at the same time I realized I was fleeing all the terrible things I had experienced.

"My sole reason to return to Vancouver for his trial was to ensure Price was convicted and sent to prison on rape charges.

"I love my job at the museum in Marseille. I was fortunate to get the internship after graduation and secure a permanent position.

"I share a flat with my best friend Céline, and I love the life I am building there."

Switching to English, asking if he would like a snack.

He follows me into the kitchen, sitting at the counter while I prepare a snack of cheese and crackers. I make coffee the European way as I brought Robusta beans from France. I use a grinder for the beans and the French press to make us two cups of coffee.

Marc smiles at me after his first sip. "A taste of home! I don't care for North American coffees or frou-frou drinks".

Observing Marc while sipping my coffee. I savour this quiet moment with this man I just getting to know better.

We just finish our coffees when Jake strides into the kitchen.

"Ok Allory," he says straight away. "We are set for UBC for eleven-thirty am and three pm at the Tea House at Stanley Park. I will drive you to UBC. And the afternoon outing.

"Jason and Willow are associates that will be in the Tea House at a nearby table.

"Marc, I suggest you bring your stuff here. I will stay here with Allory until you return. You should have enough time to get there and back before we leave for UBC as your hotel is only five minutes away."

"I will be back in in fifteen minutes."

Jake and I sit next to each other.

Jake is drumming his fingers on the counter. "How did it go? I know I threw you in the deep end."

Gripping his hand to still his fingers. "It's okay Jake. I need to have trust in the people who are going to keep me safe. Marc and I are getting to know each other.

"We spoke in French this morning which broke the ice. I made a good cup of French coffee. We have a common experience as each of us have been impacted by traffickers."

"So, he told you about his sister?"

"Yes, he did. We have shared goals to end trafficking."

"I would like us to test your GPS tracker button before we go to the UBC. I will have Leo monitor your location. Let's take a walk before Marc gets back," he suggests.

Down at street level, we walk down the block while Jake has Leo on his phone. Satisfied with the finder/locator function after walking several blocks and stopping next to buildings. Jake advises we return to the condo to wait for Marc.

Marc arrives with a small duffel bag and a few suits which he puts in a guest bedroom. He had changed into a pale pink dress shirt and black slacks with shiny black shoes.

Jake looks me and Marc over. "You will do. It is ten-thirty-five, leaving just enough time to get you to UBC for eleven-thirty."

Marc and I slide into the back seat of a black Cadillac in the parkade. There is very little conversation out to UBC.

I am astounded how much the campus has grown since I attended school here.

Before we get out at the location for the meeting, Jake tells us he will pick us up at twelve-thirty.

Aaron is a tall man with black hair and grey eyes dressed in a grey suit. He greets Marc and I at the door of his building. He shakes both of our hands after holding the door so we can enter ahead of him.

"It's a pleasure meeting you, Allory and Marc," Aaron turns to lead us to a winding glass staircase to the second floor.

We enter a large meeting room with a computer screen that dominates one whole wall. There are several people already sitting around the conference table in front of the screen. Aaron makes the introductions for Marc and me.

I begin my short presentation hoping to stimulate conversation. It was well received and created lively discussion after I finished the slides.

"Allory please email your presentation to me," Aaron requests. "I would like to share it with my boss. I will get back to you with feedback once I talk with him." We shake Aaron's colleagues' hands before leaving.

I turn to Aaron, "Thank you for making this meeting happen I was very pleased we had a good dialogue afterwards."

Aaron leads us down to the lobby, telling us he would be in touch.

With a final goodbye to Aaron, we go outside and get in the back seat of the car waiting for us at the curb.

Returning to the condo, we have a break to change into more casual clothes for the Tea House.

Marc needs to check in with his Interpol team.

I sit in the study composing a longer email to Andre giving my impressions of Aaron and his team. I add some preliminary ideas for next steps, telling him I would await feedback from him prior to planning a next meeting.

I take a chance that I will catch Céline at home as it is now one pm in Vancouver, it will be ten pm in Marseille. I call her on my cell, and I'm so happy she is home. We converse in French making me miss her more.

I tell her about my meeting at UBC and explain about Marc.

She teases me but underneath I know she is happy I have a nice guy to spent time with during this awful ordeal with Price.

I change into a soft navy dress and sandals, adding a sweater over my arm in case it gets chilly outside. I realize when I change, I need to move the GPS to the new outfit.

When I go downstairs Marc and Jake are sitting at the kitchen table talking.

They both look up when I take a seat next to Marc. "I don't want to interrupt but it is almost two forty-five. Are you ready to leave for the Tea House?"

Jake looks at his watch and nods. "You are right, it is time to go."

The drive is short with a light rain falling as we enter Stanley Park following the one-way traffic to the Tea House located to the west along the water.

Parking outside the front of the Teahouse entrance, Jake looks at us through the review mirror. "I will pick you up at five pm."

Alighting from the car, onto the sidewalk. Marc casually holds my hand and opens the door of the restaurant for me.

The maître's seats us immediately We look over the appetizers offered this afternoon. The Tea House is all windows looking out to the ocean and offering a fabulous view of the North Shore Mountains.

Choosing a lovely oak-aged Chardonnay from a local winery with an appetizer of fresh bread and red pepper jelly was a good choice.

We continue our conversation from earlier. We find we have a lot in common from snow skiing to climbing and a love of books and history.

As we linger over our wine, I casually glance around the room. I don't recognize anyone, and the place seems calm and quiet in late afternoon. I realize I can enjoy myself, despite Price's pending parole Friday morning.

Leaving the Tea House, there is a misty rain coming down. I see Jake waiting in the car. Marc opens the back door for me to get in.

Out of nowhere, a person steps close to me and snaps my picture. Marc folds me into the car, closely following me, shutting the door behind him.

Jake is talking to his team on his phone.

Finally, hanging up, he drives straight back to the condo.

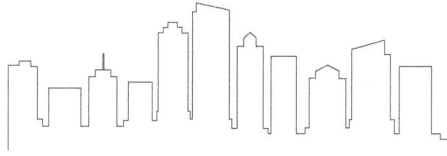

Chapter Twenty-One
Thurs late afternoon

Marc and I are silent as we sit on the sofa.

Jake takes a call from Lea. "Avery has decided to stay at her condo overnight to sleep in the comfort of her own bed."

Connor arrives right behind us. He tells us that Sean texted telling him he was running fifteen minutes late.

Going into the kitchen, I make a pot of tea puzzled why a photographer would get in my face for a picture. It's not like I am famous or anything.

Hearing the elevator arrive again, Sean strolls in. Scanning our faces.

"What happened?"

"Everything is fine. Just a blip during Marc and I's outing at the Tea House.

"A photographer got in my face, when we were leaving the restaurant, he took my picture.

"On a brighter note, my little GPS trackers work well when I was away from the condo today."

Jake provides more detail. "Our security team followed the guy to a downtown office building that houses a gossip rag. At this point we don't know why he took Allory's picture."

"Being seen around town to keep Price and his associates watching me is the goal. I am not going to worry about one picture taken by a gossip magazine.

"We've had several stressful happening in the last few days. I want us all to go out for a late dinner tonight for stress relief. I heard the Black and Blue Restaurant was good; their reviews are excellent. I will try to make a reservation around seven pm if possible."

No one disagrees.

Allory steps into the kitchen to make the call to the restaurant. As luck would have it, they had a last-minute cancellation and offered a seven-thirty reservation.

Calling Avery next, "Do you want to go to dinner at Blue and Black tonight?"

"I have been resting most of the afternoon. I have always wanted to go there. It is typically impossible to get a reservation on short notice. Count me in!"

Stepping back into the room with the guys, I update them.

"We have reservations for Jake, Marc, Connor, Sean, Avery and me for seven-thirty." I tell the boys. "Unfortunately, the security is going to have to stay out on the street as we have only one booth reserved."

"Okay" Jake nods. "Let me briefly talk about plans for Friday.

"Allory, Marc and Avery will go to lunch with the UBC friends at Neverland Tea Salon for twelve-thirty.

"In late afternoon Marc and Allory will visit the Picasso Exhibit at The Sails in Canada Place.

"Afterwards you all will reconvene at the condo to dress for the Gala at the Art Gallery. I can confirm that Price has a ticket to the event. I have organized a limousine to drive you to and from the event.

"I don't believe Price will approach you directly, Allory due to the parole restrictions. Although I guaranteed he has a plan to intimidate and scare you."

I question myself again. "Am I brave enough to be bait for Price? What choice do I have if I want my life back?"

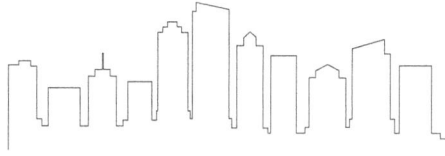

Chapter Twenty-Two
Thurs pm

Leon is escorted by the guard to a visitor area. Luis is waiting at one of the booths. A garment bag is draped behind him on the chair. Luis picks up the phone, Leon waits for the guard to step away before he picks up the phone on his side of the partition.

"Thanks for the suit and under clothing," says Price.

"No problem, boss. I have news. I heard that big sister had a car accident as she was coming back from a late afternoon meeting in the Valley. She was admitted to hospital because she was quite banged up but now is staying with Allory at the condo," he finishes with a straight face.

"Through a colleague, I understand Sean had a fire at a worksite. A shame it will put the work back months. I hear no one was seriously hurt though."

"Heard a rumour that Connor almost got run over when someone pushed him into traffic while on this way to a client meeting. I understand he wasn't injured fortunately; but it was a close call."

"Hope Avery feels better. And it is fortunate that the two brothers escaped serious injury," Leon says with a straight face.

"Glad that everything is on track for when I get home Friday. I want to celebrate by reconnecting with old friends."

"Be at the front gate by nine o'clock sharp tomorrow. Don't be late!" he warns as he hangs up the phone and signals to the guard, he is ready to go back to his cell.

The guard stops at the door to allow for Luis to hand over the garment bag. The guard unzips the bag to check it thoroughly ensuring it is just a suit and undergarments inside before he re-zips it and hands the bag to Price.

Luis leaves through the visitor's door.

Leon clenches his teeth in anger after watching the guard riffle through his garment bag. Yet another personal violation he has had to endure in prison.

Leon returns to his cell. Lying on his cot he burns with the need for vengeance!

Going back to his office, Connor hopes to clear his desk before returning to the condo to meet up with Allory, Avery, Sean, Marc and Jake for dinner.

Trying hard to concentrate, he wants to avoid replaying his near miss on Wednesday afternoon.

This morning, telling the girls what happened to him and Sean yesterday; he downplayed how much the whole incident scared him.

Now despite his resistance, the flashback unwinds slowly, pulling him in.

Preoccupied about the details from his client meeting, he and Ken are walking back to his office. Getting to the light crossing at Burrard and Alberni, the foot traffic heavy. Waiting to cross when the light turns green, suddenly someone shoves him hard from behind into the oncoming traffic. On his knees looking at a truck barrelling toward him, time stops.

At the last second before impact, Ken grabs the back of his jacket and pulls him to safety. The terrible surge of adrenalin coursing through his body then the shakes. Silently, he locks his gaze on Ken who is as agitated and pale as he is. Sitting down on the curb, we breathe heavily as the rest of the foot traffic surge around us.

"Thank you for saving my life, Ken!" Looking closely at my companion, realizing we are both wrecked for the day.

He remembers the brief call to his office to cancel the rest of his appointments for the afternoon.

Returning to his condo, he calls Jake to report the near miss; praising Ken for his quick action saving his life. For a moment, he was tempted to ask Jake to tell the girls tomorrow morning but realized he needed to break the news himself.

Sean calls after he is home. They disclose to each other what happened today. My near miss in traffic and Sean's bad news about the suspicious fire at one his worksites amounting to a thoroughly, shitty day. He offered to tell the girls about the incidents in the morning as Sean was overwhelmed trying to deal with the many issues from the worksite fire.

It was the right decision to go home yesterday having a few beers and watching a couple of innings of a ballgame. No surprise though, I had a poor sleep.

Avery and Allory were stoic hearing the news this morning, yet I knew inside they were scared because Price is messing with us.

I banish the lingering memory of my near miss to concentrate on finishing my work at the office. I arrive at the condo close to six-thirty.

Jake, Angel, Sean, Allory and Marc are at the kitchen table, when I arrive. From their grim faces he guessed that they had been talking about the fire at Sean's worksite.

Allory glances up at me with a worried look on her face when I walk in. I guess I am more transparent than I realized. Knowing Allory, she feels guilty for what happened to Sean and me.

"Price is definitely escalating, all because of me." An anguished look on her face.

Everyone is quiet for a moment, digesting the seriousness of her statement.

Connor struggles silently when his sister asks for more details.

"It was unsettling what happened yesterday, Allory, I am handling it."

Scowling, she is less than impressed with my explanation but lets it drop for now.

Divulging more detail about how I am handling my near miss won't help either of us right now.

As the eldest, his brother and sisters have relied on him to guide them in all matters pertaining to Price. I have no plans to change that by displaying how much the near miss was messing with my head.

Connor is relieved when Jake interrupts his thoughts.

"It is too much of a coincidence that Avery, Sean, and Connor have been targeted in the last two days. That means no one goes alone anywhere until this is over."

"Jake, should we be going out to dinner tonight?" asks Sean.

"Allory needs be out in the city to keep Price's attention on her. Avery's accident, Connor's near miss and your workplace fire have distracted us from our goal."

At seven-fifteen, we grab our coats as evenings are windy and cool, yet there is no forecast for rain tonight.

Walking sandwiched between Marc and Connor on the crowded sidewalk, Sean trailing behind us. The people populating the narrow walkway, returning from their workday, maybe out to enjoy the nightlife downtown.

Finding Avery, Lea and Troy waiting at the restaurant entrance; we leave our security detail outside. We press into the small street level elevator to the restaurant. We are greeted by a hostess at the entrance who instructs a waiter to seat us at our table once I gave my name.

Once settled the waiter takes our drink orders. I glance around the restaurant seeing gleaming mirrors reflecting black leather booths with lamp lighting cordoned for privacy. Each table dressed in a crisp white tablecloth and silver table settings; there are no empty tables. "Wow, the restaurant is funky no wonder it is so hard to get a reservation," I say to my companions.

Avery smirks. "I told you it was special."

Half an hour after we sit down, the waiter brings our drinks and takes our entrée orders. The food when it arrives is delicious.

Returning to remove our dishes, the waiter provides us with dessert menus. There are too many delicious desserts to choose from, so we ordered several to share amongst the six of us.

Jake casually interrupts us, "Two of Price's associates are two tables to the right."

Instead of looking, I take a moment to linger on the faces so dear to me around the table.

The edgy feeling is creeping back, knowing two of Price's men are close. Marc notices my unease, squeezing my hand under the table. I breathe out slowly remembering for now, I am safe with this group of protectors.

Marc scans the restaurant. His gaze passes over Price's two men looking for the bulge of a gun. Price could have ordered his men to harm Allory but readily dismisses that thought. Targeting her in a public restaurant would be messy and bring a lot of heat on them from the local police.

No, Price wants to punish her himself before he sells her as part of his trafficking ring.

Once dessert is finished, Sean asks for the bill. We bundle into our coats; it will have cooled down outside for the walk back to the condo.

Allory avoids looking behind her walking to the elevator, her intent to avoid catching a glimpse of Price's men. Unfortunately, the elevator door is glass, she sees two men rushing toward them before the elevator descends to the street.

The sidewalks are more crowded than when we arrived. It leaves little room for Avery to give me a quick hug, waving goodbye as she turns to the left to join Lea and Troy going in the opposite direction to the parkade.

The rest of us merging into the foot traffic in the other direction. My first instinct is to walk faster but that was impossible.

Holding Marc's hand, we navigate our way through the crowds. Soon there is less foot traffic, I consciously relax the tightness in my shoulders. Scanning the sky, lite with stars, large leafy trees swaying in the breeze along the sidewalk. The spring air, cool against my cheeks. I am taking this precious time to appreciate having my family with me.

Returning to the condo we relax in the living room; casually talking about inconsequential things.

Ken and Jase arrive to pick up Connor and Sean. Jake has a few words with his guys before they leave.

Now it is just Jake, Marc and Angel at the kitchen table.

Bidding goodnight to the trio, I head upstairs to bed.

Starting a text to Avery to ensure she got home safe; my cell phone rings with her calling.

"Just checking in that you are safe and sound at the condo.

"I just wanted to tell you I love and will see you in the morning."

"Sleep well, Avery. I will see you tomorrow." Ending the call.

I get ready for bed, falling asleep when my head hits the pillow.

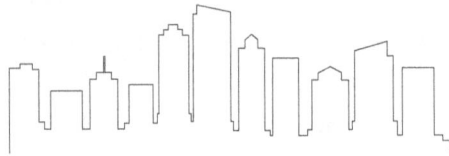

Chapter Twenty-Three
Day Four Thursday night

Price goes back to his cell from the mess hall to spend his last night in prison. He is beyond ready to be back in the world he controls.

Acknowledging to himself that raping Allory was probably a mistake. He misjudged her strength and resiliency.

She was so young and beautiful always there yet elusive. He hadn't gone to that party that night at her parents' home to rape her. It was just a lucky break he saw her come home. His plans changed in that moment. He was never satisfied with a woman that was willing. He had always got off hurting women when they couldn't fight back.

All she had to do was keep her mouth shut!

Instead, she came to court every day of his trial to ensure he went to prison.

Thinking of her, he gets hard at the memory of taking her against her will. But the ultimate power over her will be to sell her at the auction on Saturday. Then arranging her transport to Asia with the rest of the women and children that were sold. She won't be able to save herself this time by jumping into the harbour and swimming away.

He hates that he admires her gutsy courage. He won't underestimate her a third time.

He is pleased with Luis' punishment of Avery, Sean and Connor, knowing Allory would be upset and frightened. His satisfaction comes from knowing that Allory and her siblings understand he has power over them even from prison.

When he has Allory abducted this time, there will be no escape for her. Knowing Avery, Sean and Connor will be devastated, is a tantalizing thought.

Pondering, he considers abducting the sister too but quickly dismisses it with regret. He doesn't need to bring any more heat to his operations.

Reinforcing with Luis the importance of watching for and intercepting anyone hanging around the warehouse, before and after the auction on Saturday protects the merchandise. He can't have the cops find the location.

Going back to contemplating Allory's allure and her strength, he anticipates when he will break her all over again.

Yet, he remains puzzled how one small slip of a girl can take down a man of his stature and connections.

This time she won't elude him.

His intent is to ensure she remains broken this time.

A wicked smile creeps across his face, relishing what he plans to do to Allory once he is released.

Tomorrow morning dressed in his business suit. No longer shackled, he will again portray the powerful man has always been outside this prison.

Satisfied that targeting Allory's siblings achieved his purpose. She will be afraid thinking what he will do next.

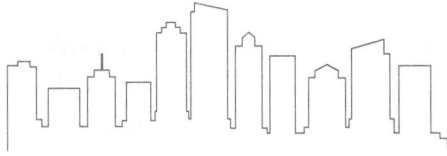

Chapter Twenty-Four
Day Five early am

Angel rubs her tired eyes at five-thirty happy to have Lea relieve her at six. She is a bit techy that surveillance is quiet. She is sure somehow Price's associates have found a way to keep an eye on the comings and goings of Allory and her siblings from here. We just can't seem to catch them at it.

I don't know how Jake is juggling his work priorities including maintaining Allory's safety.

The biggest threat today is Leon Price being released from prison this morning. The countdown has started. How and when he will come for Allory?

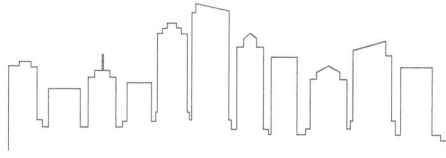

Chapter Twenty-Five
Price's parole day

At nine o'clock sharp Luis is at the prison waiting in the parking lot for his boss who will be released on parole today.

It will be good to have The Boss Man making all the decisions again. Luis is much happier carrying out orders than giving them. He has been with Price since he was seventeen. He has learned a lot from him since then.

Keeping watch towards the guardhouse, he sees Price approaching. He gets out of the car to open the back door for his boss.

Price's first words are, "Is everything set for the Gala tonight? Did you bring my cell phone?"

Luis fishes the cell phone from his pocket, handing it over to his boss before he climbs into the back seat. Luis closes the door behind him. He opens the driver's door and gets behind the wheel. He turns left out of the parking lot onto a road leading away from the prison.

"Your ticket for the Gala is on your cell phone. Teams have been set up to attend the Gala."

There is silence from the backseat as his boss focuses on his cellphone for the entirety of the trip into the city. In less than two hours Luis is pulling into the parkade of the condo building in False Creek where Price resides.

Once they enter the elevator, he pushes the button for the twentieth floor. The elevator opens into the suite showing an open concept with large floor to ceiling windows. Flooring cream-coloured ceramic tiles. A loft bedroom is at the top of a wooden staircase.

Price leads the way to his office on the left side past the kitchen. He sits down in a leather chair behind a large wooden desk dominated by his computer while Luis stands at attention waiting for his instructions.

"Order in the usual breakfast. Call the barber to come here for two pm. Arrange for the tailor to come to fit my tuxedo for the Gala at three pm.

"Luis, be back here by eleven-thirty to take me to meet my parole officer at twelve-thirty. He rattles off the address for the meeting to Luis, who enters it on his phone.

"The final instruction for now is to organize a meeting at the Club with my lieutenants for later tonight after the Gala.

"I remind you that I expect eyes on Allory every moment she is away from the condo.

"That will be all for now, Luis. Come back for me once you have made the arrangements I have requested. Remember I can't be late for the meeting with the parole officer."

After Luis leaves, the condo is quiet with no sounds from the streets below.

Leon gets up from his desk and stops in the kitchen for a plastic bag then climbs the stairs to his bedroom. He takes off the suit and underclothes he wore from the prison and puts them in the plastic bag.

Walking naked into the bathroom, he looks into the mirror over the sink, smearing shaving cream across his face and jaw. Using a smooth blade to remove his stubble. He walks over to his doorless shower and turns on the water.

Water cascades over his body. He soaps and scrubs his skin until it is reddened before rinsing and shutting off the water. He dries his body with a large bath towel. He neatly combs his hair. Looking into the mirror for a moment he sees a stranger. No red sweatshirt and pants. He has scrubbed the soiled feeling of prison from his skin. He needs no reminders of his time behind bars.

He returns to his bedroom, pulling on white underwear and undershirt. He peruses his closet for the suit and tie he will wear today.

He dons a black dress shirt, pants and suit jacket adding a crimson necktie. He puts on black silk socks with shiny black shoes. He takes a last look in the mirror at his appearance to ensure he reflects confidence and power.

Going to his top drawer of his dresser, taking his Breitling watch out of its custom case, he fastens it on his right wrist; a final sign of his power and wealth he is reclaiming.

Satisfied he leaves the plastic bag with his old suit in the bathroom for the cleaner to dispose of.

Returning downstairs, he re-enters his study on the main floor when his breakfast is delivered by security. He eats at his desk while reviewing emails and other correspondence.

The part of his brain not on business, still thinking of all the things he will do to Allory for sending him to prison. She will pay with her life for putting him away for two long years!

He relishes the many ways he will make her, and her siblings suffer. His need for revenge burned hotly inside him the entire time he was imprisoned.

Pity her parents sold their house and moved to Portugal. I could have ruined them too.

Price's thoughts are interrupted with Luis returning to take him to the meeting with his parole officer.

Listening to more detail about the conditions of his parole, he despises that he must meet with the law to maintain his parole; just another reason to punish Allory.

He tells himself to continue to play the silly little game with the parole officer, that he played while in prison. Being contrite and demonstrating remorse for his crime.

He laughs inside when the parole officer listens intently as he describes his repentance for the rape. And his willingness to meet every six weeks, setting the date for his next meeting before he leaves.

Luis takes him back to his condo where he gets a haircut and is fitted for his tuxedo for the Gala tonight. He cannot have contact with Allory due to parole restrictions, but he plans to enjoy watching his men harass and frighten her tonight.

His primary thoughts revolve around his plan to abduct Allory on Saturday, selling her at the auction with the other women and children to his buyers in Asia. This time she won't get away because he planned to put her in the container bound for Asia himself.

He calls his Club manager to review the profits for the last week.

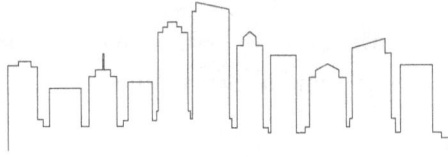

Chapter Twenty-Six
Fri morning

The next morning, waking early. Refreshed from my sleep with no nightmares, I treat myself to a long soak in the tub adding lavender oil to the water.

I feel less stressed and anxious. I need to start this day with a clean slate.

When I come downstairs Jake, Lea, Marc, Avery and I share breakfast before going over the plans for today.

"I have texts confirming lunch at the teahouse with my friends Jake.

"They know I am bringing my sister and boyfriend Marc."

My brothers arrive at ten dressed casually.

Connor stares at Avery looking at her faded bruises above her loose blouse. "You look better today. I am glad you are healing up."

Jake looks up from his MacBook asking. "Allory do you own a gun?"

"No, I don't. I have never been around firearms."

"Let's talk about it!" Jake suggests looking at Marc to include him in the conversation.

"My worry is if Allory has a gun that she could be overwhelmed before she could fire a shot. She has no experience with firearms and there is not enough time for her to become proficient," Marc cautions.

"I must agree with you Marc." Jake sighs. "It is too late to train you, so no gun!"

"Guns terrify me," Allory shutters.

Reviewing the outings for today, Jake reiterates. "It will be busy due to the planned events for lunch, the Picasso Exhibit and the Gala tonight.

"Tickets for the Exhibit have been texted to your phones, Marc and Allory.

"I will drop Allory and Marc off at Canada Place, The Sails for four o'clock to view the Picasso Exhibit. Returning to pick them up by five-thirty to dress for the Gala.

"Connor, you have all the Gala tickets on your phone to make it easier when you arrive to have one person submit them at the door.

"My understanding is there are only hors d'oeuvres and champagne at the Gala. I will order a light meal for you all before you go to the Gala.

"I will pick you up in the limousine to take you to the event by six pm and pick you up at the end of the event.

"I'm not expecting Price to abduct you at the Gala, Allory because there will be too many people there.

"My best hunch is he will wait until tomorrow night while you are out clubbing.

"It's easier at a place that is noisy and distracting for his men to snatch her right under our noses," Jake predicts.

He touches on Saturday's schedule so far.

"Allory and Marc are attending the Summer's dinner for five pm while the rest of you have a reservation for the Blue Café on Hamilton Street. After dinner you all return to the condo to get glammed up for clubbing."

"Marc and I hope to have more information later in the day on Price's activities since released from jail this morning."

Marc interrupts, "I need to leave to make my meeting with my Interpol team before we go to lunch."

Leaving at the same time, Sean and Connor return to work.

Avery looks tired. "I will lie down upstairs for a rest before we need to leave for the lunch with your friends, Allory. Come wake me up around eleven-forty so I can freshen up before we go."

"I have confidence in my crew that you will be as safe as we can make you today," Jake tells me without looking up from his computer.

Feeling a bit surreal, I'm a stranger in my own skin as I sit sipping my tea at the table where my head of security works quietly on several MacBooks.

Seeking normality. I bring my laptop to the study upstairs.

Sitting down, I check my emails. I review several draft work documents I hope to finish before we leave for lunch. At eleven-thirty I close my computer. Waking Avery to get ready for lunch.

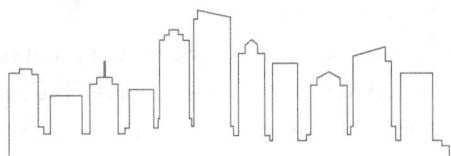

Chapter Twenty-Seven

Keeping Allory and her siblings safe, there are so many potential moving pieces almost like playing chess. Jake reminds himself that he has a great team. He continues to delegate less urgent work to others, to focus with Marc on how to tighten the noose around Price's neck.

Following Luis and other Price associates eats up a lot of his company's resources. If we can confirm Price's warehouse location and his container at the docks, we can focus on luring Price into a trap of our making.

The Port Authority has been a crucial link to have access to the docks.

Perry and Joel, my number two team has been following Price's key associates. Today they will focus on Price's activities now he is paroled.

I'm less stressed knowing Marc is with Allory today.

Thinking back on my friendship with Marc, so many memories from his years in France. Those first years away from home, living with Grand-mére Marc was always there.

He reminisces about the day they arrived at the French Army barracks in Thierville-sur-Meuse west of Verdun.

Marc from a wealthy family who owned a vineyard. Me? He was the mongrel. Part Canadian and part French, he spent more time with his grandmother in Alsace than with his parents after the divorce.

Training was harder than anything we faced aside from missions to Africa and Afghanistan.

Both of us excelled at sharp shooting and electronic surveillance. We had so much in common that it drove us to excel together. While was Marc grieving his sister, Me just messed up. We always had each other's back, though.

Missions and danger flit through my head until my memories are interrupted by Marc arriving.

Drawn out of the past, I look up when Marc sits down next to me at the table. He has a tight, frustrated look on his face.

"We're so close to connecting Price to the trafficking. My colleague Andre is accessing the Port Authority's Automatic Identification Systems and Container Tracking Devices to locate Price's container and the manifest which is the official statement of the cargo held in the container.

"He will then go after the shipping manifest, a document listing all items loaded on the vessel.

"I appreciate all the delving deep Leo did into Prices' businesses. Andre will confirm if one of Price's shell companies are linked with the manifests for the container and a vessel presently at the Vancouver docks."

"Additionally, the online auction for Saturday in Vancouver is confirmed, leaked by a Price rival," adds Jake.

"We are ninety percent confident of the location of the warehouse where the women and children are being held based on following Luis Diaz."

"Our teams are doing great Marc, but allowing Allory to sacrifice herself to get to Price is a heavy burden!

"It doesn't help me feel better that this is mostly her idea."

"I'm with you Jake, I feel the same way.

"At this point, Allory's goal is to furnish irrefutable proof he is the head of trafficking by driving him to put her in the container himself. There is a hard-core stubbornness in her that makes me think she will prevail despite fear and injury.

"Our goal although aligned with hers means taking down the entire trafficking operation including abduction, selling and transporting.

"Mounting a rescue at the warehouse could have dire consequences. We need to wait until he transports the women and children to the container to arrest him. That right now is our only viable option.

"Jake, so far, we are further ahead in this investigation because we are working together.

"Stay positive while we keep digging. We are close to having ironclad evidence that Price is head of trafficking women and children in Vancouver."

Jake knows Price will have honed his brutality in prison. How will Allory suffer when Price gets his hands on her again?

"Asking himself, can she really survive him this time?"

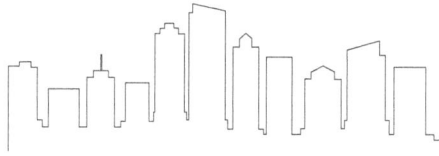

Chapter Twenty-Eight

Seeing Marc alone in the kitchen reviewing information on his cell, I am comforted by his presence.

Missing Céline and my home in Marseille, but I feel less homesick when it is just the two us.

"Why are you really involved here, Marc. I know in part because of your sister. But why here, why now?"

"Jake contacted me when your brothers hired him to protect you.

"It made sense for Interpol to pool our resources in partnership with Jake's team because he was already working with local policing."

Taking a sip of his water, He is struck with how beautiful she is with her long brown hair draped over one shoulder.

"After losing Marielle, I needed a purpose. I joined Interpol to help prevent other families experiencing what my family had endured."

"Do you think we can do that here?"

"Yes, I firmly believe together, we have the best chance to uncover Price's trafficking activities in Vancouver."

"After my experiences with Price I certainly have survivor guilt. Often especially now, I mourn the women and children that didn't escape when I did."

"The risk associated with using you to catch Price makes us all very apprehensive."

"I know. I am scared, terrified really Marc; but I must see this through to the end."

Allory takes a deep breath grabbing both of Marc's hands tightly before letting go.

"I'm going to wake Avery. She needs to dress for our lunch date with my friends. We need at least forty minutes to get across town as the traffic will be bad today."

She turns back hesitantly, "I must be honest here; it has been a while since I had a boyfriend. Be patient with me."

Changing into a dress shirt and slacks, Marc joins the girls dressed in bright spring dresses and heels carrying light sweaters and purses across their shoulders. Gallantly he offers each girl an arm.

Exiting to the parkade, Allory spies Jake leaning against his car. He opens the back door for us, we pile into the backseat.

"Tell me about your friends Allory," requests Marc.

"My friends from UBC lived with me at Gage Towers, a communal residence. The close quarters forged friendships that survived the hell of exam finals, boyfriend and girlfriend breakups, and other dramas.

"It's been harder when I moved to France to keep in touch. The last several years we've connected mostly through FaceTime. There was never enough time to really catch up with each other.

"I will tell them we met at the Museum in Marseille a month ago and you are holidaying with me."

"My cover story is I'm an architect excited to spend time with your brother Sean who has three new builds currently. I also love Vancouver from a previous visit and look forward to Allory showing me around her favorite places."

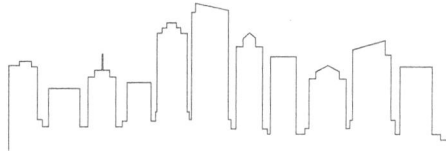

Chapter Twenty-Nine

Reaching their destination, Jake parks along the side street. Escorted to our reserved table Avery and I order tea.

My friends appear shortly after.

Jumping from my chair, I give hugs all around before introducing Avery and Marc.

Our reconnection is instant, as if we have seen each other just the other day. There are laughs, jokes.

Easily we catch up on each other's lives. Lena is a schoolteacher; Stella owns a fashion store. Taryn works for a travel company. Brent is an engineer and Michel is a lawyer. None of my friends are surprised I work at a Museum in Marseille.

Seamlessly, Marc fits in, although he listens more than contributes to the conversation. He does seem happy to talk about Marseille when asked, however, volunteers his parents own a winery and offers stories of his sailing adventures with his brother.

Equally, Avery blends in, although she is more vocal than Marc relating a funny story about her first client and her desire for a fuchsia bathroom. She was happy to share with the others when the conversation switched to travel.

When asked, she shared her most recent trip to Lord Howe Island near Australia. Even if getting there took a long time, it was well worth it.

No one is married or has kids; all of us settling into our careers. Stella and Avery make an instant connection, likely because they are both fashion designers.

The food and tea are scrumptious although the boys choose to have wine. I relax easily with old friends.

When our time together is coming to an end, my friends ask how long I will be in Vancouver. I leave it open- ended, depending on what happens with the joint project with UBC and our museum in Marseille.

There were hugs all around as we leave.

Marc, Avery and I return to the condo. Much to her chagrin, Avery acknowledges "the fatigue, aches and pains are annoyingly persistent. I will rest until we must dress for the Gala."

Marc and I relax in the living room. He talks about his brother Sebastian and relates their last sailing trip from Marseille to Barcelona which is just over one hundred and eighty-four nautical miles one way. "We were blessed with favourable winds on the way home."

"Céline and I tend to rent a small sailboat often, although we don't go far beyond the Marseille harbour."

We exchange recent climbing adventures. It is obvious Marc enjoys scaling mountains requiring more experience than I have.

"Sebastian and I climbed Mount Blanc when I was home last."

"Céline and I did the Breithorn last summer. It was spectacular."

Marc gets a text from Jake who is waiting for us in the parkade.

Parking at the drop-off point for the Sails, Jake reminds us he will return for us at five-thirty.

Entering at the main entrance, we show our electronic tickets. Leaving our coats at the check-in, I slip my purse over my shoulder.

There are people milling around the exhibit, but it is not crowded as this is the last week of the Show. Taking my hand, Marc and I walk to the first painting.

"I'm awed by Picasso, although he is not my favorite artist Marc, but I can't ignore his brilliance. I prefer Monet. Who is your favorite artist?"

"I enjoy the works of Degas," replies Marc.

Meandering around the room we spend more time at the portraits we really like, passing more quickly the art that is more esoteric in the Collection. Marc and I partake of the sparkling water and delicious appetizers set out at a table near the back.

Marc never leaves my side, close either holding my hand or casually wrapping an arm around my shoulders. He makes me feel safe and cared for.

Exiting the Exhibit, Jake is waiting at the curb. Sliding into the backseat first, Marc closing the door behind him.

Back at the condo, I'm reclining on the sofa, resting my tired feet after standing on the cement floor at the Exhibit.

I wake Avery, telling her dinner has arrived.

Once downstairs; we nibble on the food set out on the dining room table.

Heads together, Marc and Jake are sitting around the dining table discussing the reports from his team about Price's activities his first day on parole.

Jake and Marc look up when I interrupt, "I would like to discuss a strategy for us at the Gala tonight, Marc."

"I will introduce you as my new boyfriend while you carelessly scope out the other ladies at the Gala. Giving an inattentive impression, not concerned about my safety. Price and his associates will dismiss you as a threat."

"That fits with the fake identity Jake has set up for me as a rich French playboy with parents that own wineries in France."

Jake adds "according to this persona he fancies rich, connected beautiful women. If Price digs for information about him, he will find that he inherited lots of money from my paternal grandmother."

"Playing the part of a careless boyfriend hurts my heart Allory. This is not the real me who cares for you. Please remember this role is to help keep you safe, like the rest of your family and Jake's teams."

My phone is buzzing with incoming texts from Connor and Sean saying they are enroute. Their tuxedos for tonight are already here in a spare bedroom.

I join Avery upstairs after dinner to dress for the Gala.

"Avery, you have cleverly covered your bruises and scrapes with make-up. I love your hair in a high ponytail. Your green gown is beautiful with your gold shawl and shoes.

In contrast I don a cream taffeta dress with half sleeves and silver high heels. I apply light make up and leave my hair down. I add a thin silver shawl. I ensure my GPS is pinned to my dress and the other one in my small evening purse.

"Allory, we are beautiful. Let's take a picture of the two of us with your phone," Avery suggests. We crowd close taking a picture with big smiles.

We go downstairs to see our brothers and Marc in black and white tuxedos with shiny black shoes. Each one a handsome devil. Angel arrived while we were upstairs. She is gorgeous in a red dress, black stockings and low-heeled shoes.

Marc hustles us into the elevator. We get off at street level as the limousine awaits us at the curb outside the building.

Jake is driving with Lyle in the front seat dressed in a suit. "It is highly likely Price will try to somehow approach you at the Gala Allory; particularly as his associates have been dogging your steps for the last three days.

"Connor, Sean, Avery, Marc, Angel and Lyle will stick close by you at the event and will ensure you are never left alone for one minute during the Gala including needing to go to the ladies' room," Jake cautions.

Worrying about Avery overdoing it tonight, I ask her, "Are sure you can manage being in a crowd tonight?"

My sister growls at me, "I am starting to feel better. I would like to be there for you tonight, Allory. I have been resting between activities which has helped."

"Ok, but if it is too much for you, I want you to tell me, and someone can take you home."

Jake confirms that Price will be at the Gala.

"Price's residence is close by. Technically, attending the Gala doesn't contravene his parole restrictions if he doesn't have any contact with you. If his parole officer knew Price was going to be at an event that you were attending, I would think the officer would consider that Price was contravening his parole, Price is skating very close to the line.

"I have news about the trafficking ring. We have confirmed an auction on Saturday. We believe we have the location for the auction in the warehouse district near the Vancouver docks where the containers leave on ships to Asia.

"We also are hacking into the Port Authority system to confirm the location of Price's container and the shipping vessel he uses.

"After you all return from the Gala, Lea will stay to provide security tonight so Marc and Angel can get a full night's sleep. Marc and Angel will share protection duties tomorrow. I encourage you all to have a good night sleep tonight as tomorrow things will begin to ramp up.

"I need everyone to have their heads in the game from now on."

"Sean, does the fire marshal have any ideas yet of the cause of the fire at your building site?" Allory asks.

"I talked with the fire inspector today he told me he thinks it was a problem with an electrical malfunction due to the system being tampered with. I have hired night guards to prevent people entering my work sites until we get an official report from the fire inspector and WorkSafe."

Allory turns to Connor. "What progress have police made on your near miss in traffic?"

"I reported it to the police, and they have talked with Ken, but he didn't see the person who pushed me either. The police are trying to get evidence from street webcams. It is unlikely they will come up with the culprit due to the heavy foot traffic at that intersection at that time."

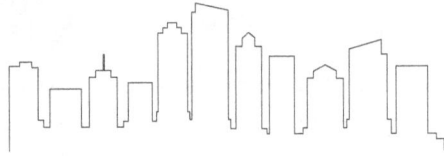

Chapter Thirty

Jake slows the limousine as we arrive at the Art Gallery for the Gala.

I look at Marc feeling jittery with nerves. He calmly takes my hand. I settle with his firm grip around my fingers. He brings my hand to his mouth for a soft kiss I feel down to my toes. A fluttery feeling settles in my stomach.

Connor is laughing at a joke Sean just told. Avery is sitting beside me, grinning at our brother Sean, the goof. He can always make us laugh.

I want to extend this carefree moment before we must play a part for the monster at the Gala.

There is a crowd arriving at the Art Gallery, most exiting from limousines like ours. Maneuvering our way through the crowd to the entrance, Connor provides our tickets to the doorman. We are ushered to the cloak room where Angel, Avery and I leave our wraps before continuing into the Gala.

The hum of multiple conversations strain against the violinist sitting playing beautiful music on his instrument in the corner to my right.

Small high tables covered with ivory tablecloths surround the ballroom that holds tonight's event. Meanwhile, waiter staff circulate around the room with champagne and hors d'oeuvres.

My understanding is the Gala tonight is to raise money for a new burn unit at Children's Hospital. Connor attends the event every year and donates to this very worthy cause.

Our plan is to gather around two round tables and have everyone come to us. The room set up will allow Marc to take an interest in other women in the room. While I am protected by having my brothers close.

I know Jake has placed several of his team amongst the patrons that continue to flow into the room from the entrance.

Although I know Marc's wandering eyes looking at all the beautiful women is a role he is playing; I have a heavy heart watching him do it.

The evening progresses with no sign of Price. At two hours I start to wonder if he really will make an appearance, when I feel a stir in the crowd.

Casting my gaze at the entrance I see Price looking directly at me. His smile haunts me. I feel goosebumps travel down my body. He merges seamlessly into the crowd.

Remaining close to my siblings, I work to act natural. For the next half hour, it seems I'm successful, until I sense someone approaching me from behind. I turn to look over my shoulder, startled by a dark-haired man in a tuxedo standing immediately behind me.

I don't know him, but his dark gaze gives me shivers. I turn to face him as he steps closer. I instinctively step back bumping into Avery while the man continues to stare at me. "Mr. Price sends his regards, Allory." After delivering his message, he turns away and is quickly lost in the crowd.

Connor takes a step to follow him. "Connor don't!" I grab his arm.

Sean looks like he wants to do something too but restrains himself when I shake my head at him. I exhale my held breath when my brothers stay at the table with me.

Marc leans down to drop a soft kiss on my cheek while folding his arm through mine. We start circling the room. We stop every few minutes to look at each displayed piece of art in the gallery, pretending we are enjoying ourselves.

Marc continues to alternate between being attentive to me and scrutinizing all the beautiful women we pass.

My brothers and sister work the room but manage to stay close at the same time. The three-hour Gala seems endless.

I catch an occasional glimpse of Price surrounded by a local up incoming politician, businessmen, women and a few elite athletes. His recent criminal history seems to only bother me.

Finally, it is time to leave. It is very crowded when we go to the cloakroom to get our wraps.

Suddenly Price's associate appears in front of me again. This time blocking me from leaving as he holds my gaze for a long moment. I feel trapped until

Marc is there holding me tightly to his side moving me toward Connor, Sean and Avery who are standing off to the left.

When I look over my shoulder the man has disappeared. I realize Price is telling me he can get to me anywhere, anytime.

Guiding me into the limousine with his hand on my low back, Marc sits next to me. I start to shake as I hold his hand in a death grip.

Once Connor, Sean and Avery are seated in the back, Jake pulls away from the curb. We are silent returning to the condo.

Walking out of the elevator Angel, Avery and I take off our wraps.

Avery and I go upstairs to remove our dresses, putting on our pyjamas and robes.

When we return downstairs Jake is standing in the living room silently, looking out at the darkened harbour view. Sean, Marc and Connor have changed out of their tuxedos.

Angel has also changed into jeans and a t-shirt resuming her surveillance duties including, debriefing with Lea.

"Well, what can I say?"

"Price is obviously not bothered, nor are all his friends at the Gala that he is a criminal paroled just this morning. He is testing us to see our weaknesses."

"Yeah," mutters Connor with a dark scowl. "To have his associates approach you in the crowd twice is very unnerving."

Jake looks around the room at each of us.

"Price's associates attended the Gala for the express purpose to frighten you. Price is paying lip service to his parole restrictions, sending his men in his stead. I am sure he was somewhere in the ballroom enjoying your reaction to his men.

"The outings tomorrow will push Price to act. He must snatch you, Allory before the auction scheduled tomorrow night if, as we believe his intent is to include you in the auction.

"I have a man discretely following Price when he leaves his condo. He hasn't been tagged yet. If Price and his men aren't vigilant, they may not spot him.

"You all need to try to get a good sleep because tomorrow is the day we end this standoff with Price."

Before Jake leaves, he has a few words with Angel.

Avery and I hug Connor and Sean before they go.

Avery and I share the bathroom, bumping into each other brushing our teeth.

I stick my tongue out at her, and she pushes me into the shower door.

Giggling, I make a ghoulish face at her.

Being silly with my sister, I start to settle after the encounter with Price's men.

I ask her if she wants to take a pain pill to help her sleep. "No, I am so tired I will be asleep almost before my head hits the pillow."

We part at her bedroom after I give her a fierce hug. "Thank you for being there tonight. You are the best sister ever!"

"Night Allory. See you in the morning." She leaves the door slightly ajar.

I know I am not ready to sleep. I put on my bathrobe and go back downstairs.

I curl up on the sofa next to Marc after turning on the electric fireplace and grabbing the blanket from the chair. I am still chilled after returning from the Gala.

He pulls me close, wrapping his arm around my shoulders.

The silence between us is soft and easy. In this moment I feel safe.

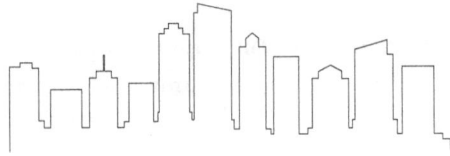

Chapter Thirty-One

My distress at seeing Price at the Gala wanes, leaning my head on Marc's shoulder. Realizing I am suddenly exhausted. I think I will be able to sleep now.

"Goodnight Marc, see you in the morning. Thank you for being a safe place to unwind after what happened at the Gala."

"Sleep well Allory. See you in the morning," Marc replies.

Once upstairs I fall into bed, asleep instantly. Another of my recurring nightmares of Price abruptly intrudes.

It is two weeks after Price is charged with sexual assault. He was granted bail as he was deemed to not be a flight risk, nor high risk to the community; detention was not needed because he agreed to appear in court for his pending trial.

The evening of a friend's birthday party, we are at L'Abattior in Gastown.

Planning all along that I would leave early, I had to meet my tutorial group tomorrow at eight am. My plan, to Uber back to Gage Towers. The party was still in full swing, but I was tired, and my feet hurt in my new high heels.

When I get a text that my ride was almost here, I exit to the street, waiting near the door on the sidewalk.

The Uber is half a block away just pulling around the corner.

Abruptly, I'm grabbed from behind. A large hand over my mouth preventing me from screaming. Dragged around a dark corner to our left, shoved into an open trunk that is slammed shut above me. The vehicle drives a short distance before stopping.

The trunk opens, I glimpse my abductor for the first time. He is a tall heavy-set man. He drags me out of the trunk, despite my struggles to break free, I am forced down a dark staircase through a door at the bottom.

He shoves me roughly down an ill-lite hallway. He opens a door to our right and pushes me into a dark room. I hear him lock the door behind me. I still had my purse with my cellphone, but something is blocking the signal to call out.

Not knowing how long I sit on that dirty floor shivering in the dark. I hear the click of the lock. Standing in the doorway is Price with a wicked smile on his face. He walks into my cage closing the door and turning on an overhead light.

I am trembling with fear and dread. His handsome looks hide the monster inside of him. This animal who tied me up and raped me in my own bed at home where I should have been safe. He shattered my sense of security and subjected me to pain and trauma. And worse I lost myself for a time.

"You clearly didn't listen to me when I told you to tell no one about the night I visited you during your parents' party. Now you dare to accuse me of rape. You need to be punished," he says in a deadly quiet voice.

Suddenly he grabs me brutally by the hair and lifts me from the floor. He slaps me so hard across the face my ears are ringing. He drops me to the floor and kicks me several times against my ribs and back. I gasp for air.

"You are a small problem that will be gone tonight," he says contemptuously while picking up my purse and opening the door. As Price storms out, he instructs someone in the hallway to put her in the holding cell with the rest of the girls.

A large ugly man grabs my arm and drags me out of the room and down the hallway. He stops at a door, unlocking it shoving me to the floor. I listen to the clang of the door shutting and click of the lock.

Hearing other people in the room with me, some silent, others sobbing quietly. I ache from the beating Price gave me, realizing resting is impossible.

I don't know how long it is before men come to take us away. They bind our hands and blindfold us, forcing us to walk until a soft breeze likely an open door is in front of us. They force us to climb into the back of what I suspect is a large truck then close and lock the doors once all of us are inside.

I take off one of my shoes and push the spike heel through the tie holding my wrists together, it breaks. I put my shoe back on. I lift a corner of the blindfold enough to see details. I'm in a truck with other women and children that look terrified.

I think we travel for less than thirty minutes when the truck stops. I hide my bound hand over the one that is free.

I can smell the ocean and hear the waves slapping the docks as the two guards open the back doors. They have guns and drag us roughly into a single file out of the back of the truck. Driving us to walk toward what looks like an open cargo container.

I knew I had one chance to escape, waiting for it. When several girls get tangled together and tumble to the ground. I take my chance. While the guards turn to them, I tear off my blindfold and leap for the water.

I dive deep as one guard starts shooting, I hear the bullets hit the water. One grazed my right arm. I continued to swim deeper thankful of my synchronized swimming training that enabled me to hold my breath under water for long periods of time.

When I no longer hear bullets or boats on the water, I decide it is safe to surface. My lungs almost bursting, I cautiously peek my head out of the water, noting I am a long way from the dock. The water is freezing, and I am shivering, now worried about hypothermia.

Wrenching my head to the west seeing the lights of the Heli jet pad. I swim as quickly as I can, reaching a ladder that extends from the water to the Heli jet pad above.

My hands are numb from the cold. I fumble when I try to grab the first rung of the ladder. I rub my hands together briskly then try again. Pulling myself one rung at a time to the top of the ladder, rolling exhausted on to the pad surface.

After a few minutes trembling with the cold, I force myself to stand, I lost my shoes in the ocean, anticipating a painful walk to find shelter.

Limping along Waterfront Street most shops closed with darkened windows. I don't know how long it took to reach a corner store two blocks away. I count my blessing it's open.

The storekeeper allowed me to use his phone to call Connor and gave me a hot cup of tea and blanket while I waited.

I must have made some noise in my sleep because when I wake from my nightmare, the bedside light is on, and Avery is lying next to me holding my hand. No words are needed as my sister is the keeper of all my night terrors.

It isn't easy to shed the horror of the night Price exposed me to human trafficking, knowing I'm going to let it to happen again.

I turn to hug Avery. Deflecting from me.

"How are you really doing since your car accident?"

"Allory I am doing much better each day. If I'm having nightmares I don't remember them. She admits she has aches and pains and more headaches than usual.

"The fatigue is still a problem but resting during the day makes it manageable."

Avery spends the early morning hours talking with me about her business to take my mind off the nightmare. Every moment I spend with my sister is precious. I refuse to allow Price to steal one moment of this early morning together.

Telling me she will take a nap she returns to her room; she will come down for breakfast around eight-thirty am.

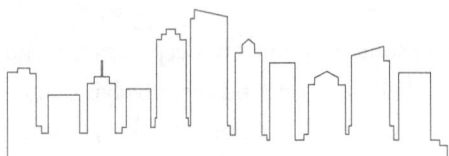

Chapter Thirty-Two

After Avery leaves, I lie in bed for a few minutes accepting the inevitable reality of this pivotal Saturday when Price will abduct me again. I choose the confrontation with Price this time, because I want my life back. I want to ensure he can never sell woman and children for profit again.

Going downstairs I find Lea monitoring surveillance at the kitchen table. She tells me Jake will be here by eight am to talk about plans for today.

I sit visiting with her. "My niece is coming to spend the weekend with me in two weeks to give my sister a break before the arrival of her second child."

"How old is she?" I ask.

'She is five years old and a real kick," Lea tells me with a huge grin.

"I'm going start a pot of coffee for Jake and prepare French Press for Marc. Do you want anything Lea?" "No thanks Allory, if I have caffeine now, I won't be able to sleep," she replies.

I'm pouring water into the coffee pot when Marc strolls into the kitchen.

"How did you sleep Allory?"

I pause for a moment. "I had a nightmare about my last abduction. I woke to see Avery holding my hand."

Marc pulls me to him for a hug. "If you can't escape him this time, know that we will prevent him from smuggling you out of Vancouver."

A few minutes later Jake is walking into the kitchen, he looks very tired. "Didn't you sleep last night?" I ask, perusing his rumpled appearance.

"I was up late getting updates from the teams. I will brief you all once Connor arrives. Sean called me, he will be here this afternoon after his meeting at a worksite."

"How is Avery doing?" he asks. "She looked exhausted last night after the Gala."

"I left her upstairs sleeping. I am worried about her fatigue level. She assures me she is getting better each day."

Jake goes to check in with Lea.

Checking on Avery, she is still sleeping. I wake her and tell her to come down when she is ready for breakfast.

Jake and Marc are in the kitchen with Connor. Avery joins us looking more rested.

Sitting around the table together for breakfast, we are quiet with our thoughts.

"I understand that Connor thinks you all should go sailing this morning and lunch at Jericho Beach," Jake informs us.

Marc, Avery and I perk up, enthusiastically agreeing with Connor's plan.

Jake reviews other plans for today.

"I will drive Allory and Marc to Aaron Summers' house for dinner at five pm and pick them up when they text me to return.

"Connor, Avery, and Sean have a dinner reservation for five pm at the Blue Café. "Lea and Angel will go with them to provide security while the second team, Troy and Ken; do reconnaissance outside.

"After dinner everyone will return to the condo to get glamourous for clubbing."

Jake finishes discussing the plans with a warning to each of us to stick close to our security details today especially Allory and Avery.

"Price could be considering abducting both of you, if an opportunity presented itself."

Allory gives her sister a fearful look. They had not thought of that possibility before.

To break the tension I ask, "I hope you have left me, Avery and Angel at least an hour to get glamourous after the UBC dinner and before clubbing," I tease Jake.

"No worries I appreciate that the wardrobe changes take time. I have given you plenty to get ready," he reassures me with a wide grin.

"Price will be very interested to know where you are today, Allory," he continues.

"I acquiesce Jake, not without fear but hoping Price's plans go awry."

Avery interrupts. "When do we leave for the yacht club? It is a gorgeous day; I can't wait to go sailing.

"Sean is going to be very envious that we are going sailing without him. He told me yesterday; he needs to play nice with the crabby building inspector who is coming to one of his construction sites today."

After changing into yoga pants, long sleeved t-shirts and fleece jackets for sailing we join the guys.

"Let's go people," Connor orders heading to the elevator.

"See you later Lea," I say with a wave.

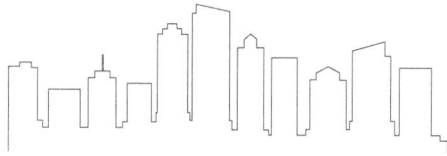

Chapter Thirty-Three

Crowding into the elevator, I'm happy to be pressed close to Marc. Jake left us a company car to drive today.

Connor takes the wheel. Avery climbs into the passenger side. Marc and I settle in the backseat. He holds my hand as I put my head on his shoulder.

When we exit the parkade, the skies are blue with fluffy white clouds in the distance.

Connor turns off Georgia onto Burrard Street leading to the old bridge over the inlet.

Marc and I being history buffs, I detail some facts about the bridge's history. "This old Art Deco style, steel truss bridge across the inlet was built over two years between nineteen thirty and nineteen thirty-two.

"Wow this bridge is old for North American standards then? Marc asks."

"Yup. It can't compare to the bridges in Europe though, ages ahead of us."

Turning my head to look at the ocean to our right, "it looks perfect for sailing today and I can't wait to be on the water."

"I made reservations for two sail boats that will be waiting for us at the dock when we arrive," explains Connor.

Exiting off the bridge onto Fourth Avenue toward Jericho Beach Connor is looking in the rearview mirror. He sees the security detail followed by another car. He keeps this information to himself.

Reaching the yacht club, Connor turns right into the parking lot.

"Everyone out boys and girls. It's show time," Connor orders.

Avery grabs our loaded back packs from the trunk. "Snacks and stuff to have a fun sail, that Connor organized," she says with a laugh.

"We are in two boats because Jericho has only smaller boats for rental," interjects Connor.

Donning our lifejackets. I jump in with the pack while Marc pushes the boat offshore. Connor doing the same with Avery. It is a beautiful day with a steady wind.

Soon we are skimming the waves. Marc leans the boat into the wind with Connor doing the same alongside us as we head out of the harbour. There is something so freeing as the boat speeds forward,

leaving the shore far away.

Relaxing, I watch Marc turning us into the waves. I can hear Avery laughing at something Connor says as they speed past us. The race is on. Marc has sailed many times before, smiling as he and Connor try to out distance each other. Reclining in the seat, I bask in the sunshine.

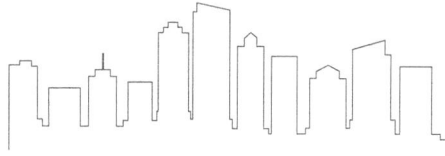

Chapter Thirty-Four

We are out for several hours. Sooner than I wish Marc and Connor turn us back toward the marina. When we reach the dock, the guys tie the boats, and we adjust to our land legs.

Walking as a group to the yacht club, Connor gives his name to the reservation desk. We are swiftly seated at our table overlooking the harbour. We make a silent pact to ignore everything but each other.

The waiter arrives to take our orders. It's obvious that Connor and Avery find Marc good company. He is witty and charming and able to hold his own with Connor.

We take our time over the splendid meal with much laughter. Marc has his hand on my thigh drawing small circles that are driving me crazy, but I have no desire to stop him.

Finally, it is time to leave. Connor deals with the cheque.

Avery and I head to the ladies' room. Exiting the bathroom, the corridor is blocked by two of Price's associates. They just stand and look at me without saying anything. I'm shaken by their proximity.

Our security detail pushes them aside and leads Avery and me to the car, where the guys wait.

"Price is pushing the limits" I say to the guys. "His cronies were waiting for us when we were leaving the bathroom. They blocked the entrance despite our security standing there, waiting."

"We expect this kind of behaviour. But I don't think Price has directed his associates to abduct you in broad daylight with lots of witnesses present," Marc explains.

It's quiet in the car after that. Marc slips his arm around my shoulder. A warmth along my side when the rest of my body is cold.

Arriving at the condo Avery and Connor sit visiting with Lea.

I go into the kitchen to get a glass of water giving myself an alone moment.

Marc walks in after a few minutes, sliding an arm around my waist. "En française, veux-tu parler?"

His question takes me away from here. He and I quietly converse in French. I can feel my tense muscles letting go.

Reclaiming our seats with the others, Avery has a thoughtful look on her face as she watches me and Marc.

My sister would never ask what was going in front of Lea. She will wait to corner me later.

"So how did the sailing go Allory?" asks Lea.

"It was gorgeous on the water with just enough wind to make it perfect. I forgot how much I love to sail!"

Laughing, Avery teases. "Next time the boys can sit back and relax as we take the keel." Connor raises a skeptical eyebrow and Marc just grins.

We have the luxury of some free time in early afternoon to do just nothing.

Avery joins me upstairs when it's time to dress for dinner.

She wears a white t-shirt with fancy jeans and boots.

I change into a blouse and lavender skirt slipping on sandals, asking Avery to braid my hair.

Going downstairs, we find Connor, Sean and Marc in the living room.

Angel has arrived sitting with Lea at the kitchen table.

Marc and I say hello to Sean and Angel before we leave for the Summers' dinner.

The dinner at Aaron's is very relaxing and the meal is delicious.

The colleagues Aaron has invited attended my presentation at UBC. We have a lively debate with some new ideas bandied around with how to move forward with our partnership.

Marc texts Jake when we are ready to leave.

Aaron and his wife walk us to the door. "Thank you for the fabulous meal and great company. Aaron, talk soon."

Heading back to the condo, Marc and I compare impressions of the dinner. I'm hopeful that a partnership with UBC and the Marseille Museum comes to fruition.

I lean into Marc during the ride. A poignant moment where I feel totally safe.

Jake, Marc and I find Connor, Avery and Sean beat us back to the condo.

Raving about the food at the restaurant tonight, Avery encourages us to try it out at another time.

Angel will join us clubbing for extra support meanwhile Lea will maintain a broader digital surveillance connected to Leo at Jake's office.

"Thoughts on tonight," Jake asks Allory.

"I can't think ahead Jake, or I will be paralyzed with fear. You suspect I will be abducted tonight; I agree.

"I must let it happen and endure what Price does to me. I wish you could rescue me from the warehouse, but we can't risk the other women and children.

"How are the Button GPS trackers working Jake?"

"To this point, we have not lost reception. Our team has been able to locate you everywhere you have been in the city.

"Allory, once you are abducted, I am sure they will search for trackers and destroy them. We will have a starting point to follow wherever Price has instructed his men to take you."

"I admit that freaks me out, but it is part of the deal."

I shake my head at Connor, knowing he is considering pulling me out of this. That will never be an option I can live with.

Jake interrupts Connor and I's staring contest.

"There will be two of my teams tracking you at each club.

"Connor, Sean, and Avery you will have tough roles tonight. To end this, you must be prepared for the reality that Allory will be abducted.

"My best guess is when Allory leaves the table to go to the bathroom.

"Price has instructed his associates to grab her. I will have Jensen hidden close to witness the abduction while Jensen's partner, Eric will wait to tail the vehicle that Allory is abducted in."

"They will follow you Allory to confirm the location of the warehouse where Price will hold the auction. But they can't interfere until you and the other women and children are transported to the docks.

"At this point, tying Price to trafficking means arresting him when he brings the women and children to the docks, to transfer them into his container.

"We have eyes on the confirmed shipping container and its location at the docks matching the manifest registered to one of Price's shell companies.

"After the auction, when women and children are sold to foreign buyers, Price and his associates have arranged transport from the warehouse to the docks to load them in the container set to sail to Asia tonight.

"I had our profiler anticipate Price's actions. She tells me that Price will personally deal with Allory and ensure she doesn't escape this time.

"Both my team and Interpol will be at the docks to intercept Price and his colleagues.

"Any comments or suggestions?" Jake scans the room, taking time to look at each of us. There is no active dissent seen.

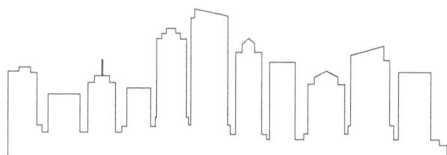

Chapter Thirty-Five

The girls and Sean remain in the living room to visit, while Jake, Marc and Connor sit down at the kitchen table with Angel and Lea.

"Any other comments?"

"We know this is going to happen Jake. But damn, this is my baby sister! There are so many things that could go wrong. It doesn't help that I know if we don't get Price, Allory will never be safe. I hate feeling helpless," grounds out Connor.

Jake empathizes with Connor. "Allory wants her life back. Now Price is on parole his priority tonight is to ensure Allory is locked tight in his container bound for Asia."

Hanging his head, Connor takes several deep breaths. He looks at Marc who sits quietly next to him. "Marc, any comments?"

"This is difficult for all of us. None of us would choose her to be bait. She doesn't see any other alternatives.

"Ending this monster's domination of her life, that is the end goal."

Marc goes on to explain the role of his team tonight to Connor.

"If Price uses lethal force, we will call for additional supports from the local authorities. For now, we are circling the lion to re-cage him."

Marc leaves to do a last check in with his Interpol team.

Jake talks with Lea and Angel.

Connor joins his family in the living room.

Sean is really bummed he missed out on sailing this morning.

He suggests they plan a trip to Whistler after Price is dealt with.

"I could bring my mountain bike. Connor, you and the girls could rent bikes at the Mountain.

"Even better we could take a Whistler River rafting trip," he says enthusiastically.

Avery interrupts him. "I think we could go on the Whistler Tasting Tour that is a guided walking excursion to four restaurants in the Village."

Marc and Jake join us after talking with their teams while we set aside our ideas for a trip to Whistler.

They have us all laughing over their crazy stunts they pulled when Jake lived in France. It dispels some of the fear for a short time.

Allory and Avery decide to go upstairs for some sister time. They lie on Allory's bed facing each other.

"I think I will wear my blue slinky pant suit to go clubbing tonight so I can wear lower heels that I can run in if needed.

"All this changing wardrobe is exhausting," she moans.

Avery frowns, "I wish I could be as calm as you are right now."

"But I'm not! I am scared Avery.

"I want my life back! At this point our plan is my only viable option to ensure he can no longer hurt women and children again."

With nothing more to say, Avery changes the subject.

"So…let's talk about Marc. That is a more interesting conversation . . ."

"Oh, that man is gorgeous," sighs Allory.

"We can talk about anything. I love he is French and comes from a good family. We have lots in common from sailing to climbing. We both have tight family units."

Allory blushes. "He is a great kisser too".

"I knew it," Avery sighs. "I have seen the way he looks at you. Once tonight is over, you can see where this goes with him."

"I really hope so!

"It's likely time to dress for tonight's clubbing."

There is a knock on the door.

Allory sees Angel poke her head in when she opens the door. "Room for another gal to get glammed up?" Angel has her dress over her arm.

The three of us crowd into the bathroom to share the mirror applying our make-up and styling our hair.

Avery wears a short black shirt with a cream blouse with black stockings and heels. I'm in my sparkly blue pantsuit with low heels. Angel is sleek in a short orange sparkly sheath with black high heels showing off her fabulous, toned legs.

I get us close to take some pictures on my phone of our glamourous look.

"Give me a few minutes," I ask Avery when we are ready. She gives me a tight hug before her and Angel go downstairs.

For a few minutes I lie across my bed, I imagine I am a fluffy white cloud traveling across a bright blue sky - no worries, no fears, no anticipation of bad things to come. It is a moment in time. Allowing the jitters to settle inside me. I take deep breaths, relaxing my tight muscles. I'm just here, drifting.

There is a soft knock on the door before it opens. Marc is standing in the doorway.

"Can I come in for a moment?"

"Sure!"

He takes a seat on the bed next to me. "You look like you are in the zone."

"Funny you say that; I was just floating as a fluffy white cloud."

He strokes a finger down my cheek, then leans over and kisses me deeply. He looks into my eyes, and I melt as he trails his fingers down my arm.

"We will have time after this is over, Allory. You have become very important to me. I want to see where this takes us." After another luscious kiss on my mouth. He gets up.

"I will see you downstairs. If I don't leave now . . ." he grins.

"See you soon," closing the door behind him.

I lie there thinking about Marc with a silly smile on my face.

I take a further ten minutes to bolster my courage to face Price again.

I head downstairs. I take a seat on the sofa next to Marc. Everyone is now dressed in party clothes.

Sean is laughing at Connor as he beats him badly at crib while Avery eggs them on. Angel is talking to her girls on her cell.

It is now seven pm and the clubs will begin filling up.

"Show time folks," says Jake. We get our coats and head to the elevator.

"Even when you are alone and scared know we are going to get you back from Price, Allory," Jake promises.

It is a short drive to the first Club.

Sean gives us a lowdown of his week dealing with a cranky building inspector at his new build on the Westside. Sean knew he was up to code. Fortunately, everything passed inspection.

"I will be happy when this old conger retires. We have always rubbed each other the wrong way pretty much since the first time he came to inspect one of my buildings.

"Sailing certainly would have been more fun," he says with a grumpy look on his face.

I wrap my arm around his neck for a hug. He hugs me back harder. No words needed.

We arrive at the entrance of the first club, Levels. Jake has arranged a table in the VIP area. We will go to the next club Bar None and then Price's club Dominos if needed.

We step out onto the sidewalk. I take my phone from my purse. I ask Angel and Avery to stand close as I take several more pictures of us, gorgeous and glamourous. Then one of the boys, handsome in dress pants with shiny black shoes and white dress shirts with black jackets but no ties.

"We look good," admires Connor.

Passing through the main entrance of Levels in single file minutes later, the music is loud. Connor raises his voice to the doorman for directions to the VIP area. The man grabs a passing server to direct us.

We are led to a seated area above the dance floor.

A waiter arrives to take our drink orders. "Connor get me a pitcher of ice water. I need to keep my wits about me."

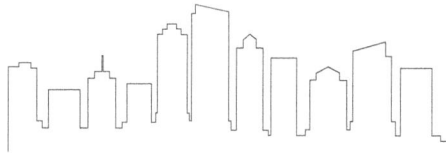

Chapter Thirty-Six

The DJ is good, and I enjoy the music. About a half hour after we arrive, I tell Angel I need to go to the bathroom. She is wearing a mic to communicate with the rest of Jake's team and lets Jensen know I am going to the loo. I give Avery a brief hug in passing.

I leave my purse on the table and follow the signs to the washroom. I don't see Jensen but that is the whole point.

I reach the door, feeling a prickle at the back of my neck.

I look behind me. A tall, dark man is now standing outside the men's room next to the ladies. He draws a gun from behind his back and steps toward me. In a panic I try to run but he is closer than I expected. He grabs my arm. I scream but no one else is in the corridor.

Motioning with his gun for me to keep walking ahead of him down the corridor where it turns left with another door announcing the exit.

Grabbing my upper arm hard enough to bruise. I decide I won't make it easy for him and try to kick and hit him. He smacks me hard enough against my head I feel dizzy.

I am a ball of fear, anger and terror for what is coming next.

Dragging me out a door to an alleyway, there is a dark car sitting idling. The guy takes out an electronic device and sweeps it over my clothes. Plucking off my Button GPS, he smashes it under his shoe.

Shoving me roughly toward the open door into the backseat. I resist but its futile because he is so much stronger than me. He slams the door shut. Getting in the front seat with the driver who automatically locks all the doors in the vehicle when I try to open my door.

We drive for about twenty minutes and stop. The tall dark, dangerous guy opens the door and drags me onto the crumbling pavement of a driveway in front of a large, weathered warehouse. I resist when he grabs my arm. He slams his fist into my chest. I can't breathe for a moment it hurts so bad.

He drags me down a rickety set of stairs, unlocks the door at the bottom and drags me down a dark corridor that opens to a wide space that has cages on either side. I can see terrified faces looking out as we continue to the end of the corridor.

He unlocks an empty cage and shoves me in, re-locking the door behind me. I stumble and fall hard to my knees. I sit there hearing the soft sobbing of another caged person close to me. It is so hard to believe this will go well for me. I shiver with cold and despair.

———◆———

Jensen alerts Angel and Eric through their mics. "Allory was taken at gunpoint outside the ladies' bathroom," he reports. "He is taking her through the back-alley entrance now."

"I see them in the alley," interrupts Eric. "She is being pulled forcefully toward the back of a black car by a tall dark guy. He swept her for trackers. He found her Button tracker, removed and crushed it under his shoe before he shoved her in the back seat."

Jensen jumps into the passenger's seat, his door not all the way closed before Eric speeds after the car with Allory.

"We are following at a discrete distance. Our GPS is on so you can track our car. I can't see the license plate on the car we are following because it is blacked out."

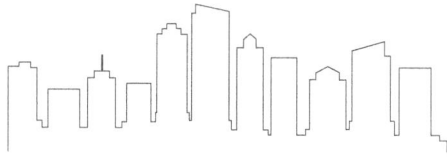

Chapter Thirty-Seven

Jake leaves his parked car and enters the Club. He makes his way to the VIP lounge where Connor, Sean, Avery, Marc and Angel sit waiting. He confirms that Allory has been abducted.

"I will take you all to the condo and leave Angel and Lea with you.

"Marc and I have teams converging at the docks where Price's container is located.

"Eric and Jensen are following the car Allory was abducted in. From GPS tracking it looks like they are headed to the warehouse we identified as owned by Price."

He brings the car around to take Angel, Connor, Sean and Avery to the condo until they get Allory back. Marc opens the trunk to get his change of clothes he had stowed there.

Minutes later a dark car slows down next to Jake. Marc gets in the front seat.

"See you at the docks."

Connor gives Jake a long look before getting in the backseat with Avery and Sean. "We will get her back Connor! You need to hold it together for Avery and Sean. Don't break on me now! Your baby sister is strong and smart. We will get her back!"

Meanwhile, Marc is enroute to the docks. He sends a text to his team leader with his ETA. Jake and Marc's team are connected by an intercom system to ensure timely communication though this crisis. Part of Jake's men are already at the docks.

Marc's team has been working with the Port Authority for weeks to set up surveillance and delving into how Price was accessing the docks.

Tonight, all employees on nightshift were sent home being told that there was a hazardous spill that needed to be dealt with quickly to ensure no spillage went into the ocean or harmed workers.

They posted an armed Port Authority guard behind a barricade at the gate to prevent anyone aside from Marc and Jake's teams through onto the docks. Marc will leave one of his team members with the guard for support.

The Port Authority with assistance from Marc's team earlier today confirmed the container location on the dock based on digital confirmation and the manifest clearly tying Price's involvement in human trafficking through the Port.

While Marc is arriving at the docks, Jake updates Alloy's siblings as he drives them to the condo.

"Jensen has checked in. He and Eric have the car Allory was abducted in within sight. Eric has a sophisticated GPS in the car to enable Leo to track them from the office."

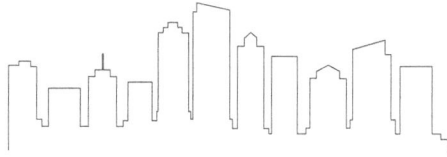

Chapter Thirty-Eight

Eric follows the car with Allory speeding away from the club determined not to lose them. They leave the downtown taking the shortest route to the warehouse district and docks.

"I don't want to get too close, Jensen because they could spot us!"

Eric tries to keep at least two cars behind them, worried when the traffic starts thinning, he lags a bit further behind the car they are following.

After twenty minutes the car slows to enter a driveway to a large warehouse.

Eric drives past the warehouse dropping Jensen on a darkened corner with no lights.

Stealthily, Jensen makes his way back to the warehouse finding an ideal dark corner to watch. Through his night goggles he sees Allory in her blue pant suit being dragged out of the car resisting her captor until he slams his fist into her chest.

The brute holding her drags her down the stairs and enters the building. There is nothing more to see after Jensen watches for a further ten minutes.

Eric parks the car in a shadowed alley close to the warehouse with a view of loading dock.

Meanwhile Jensen is making his way back to Eric as it is now full dark.

He joins him in the shadowed alley, both training their night vision goggles on the loading dock waiting. It is several hours that the two men watch and wait.

At two-thirty am a large panel truck arrives and backs into the loading dock. Three guys get out of the truck and enter the warehouse through the same door Allory was taken through.

After ten minutes, Jensen begins to see women and children being loaded into the truck. He spies one man carrying a woman in a blue pant suit.

Jensen and Eric withdraw silently to avoid detection. They climb into the car silently. Eric, keys his mic, speaking in a whisper.

"This is the right place. They are loading the women and children. I saw Allory loaded into the truck, it appears she can't walk on her own,"

It is close to three am when the panel truck leaves the loading dock, followed closely by a red Ferrari.

Jensen keys his mic, "Jake there is a red Ferrari following the panel truck. I think it's Price."

"Eric needs to follow the truck and the Ferrari but far enough behind, so they don't spot you," Jake orders.

"Roger that boss!" Jensen turns off his mic.

They waited a further five minutes before following the truck and likely Price in the car obviously headed in the direction of the docks.

"We need to stay further behind the Ferrari because there is almost no traffic on either side of the road now. I don't want him to spot us because we need him to go to the docks," cautions Eric.

Jensen updates Jake, "We are hanging back a little further as there is no other traffic, we want to avoid being spotted by Price."

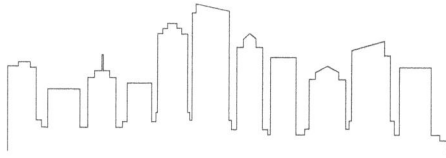

Chapter Thirty-Nine

Cold and scared, there is limited light. I don't know how long I have been sitting on the cold cement floor. The sounds I hear are the other women and children in the cages close by.

Suddenly there is a beam of light shining in my cage. Although I can't see the person clearly, I know it's Price. He unlocks the door and enters.

He stands over me with silent menace. A tall dark intimidating figure from my nightmares. I look at him silently refusing to shake.

"You have a lot to account for Allory. Putting me in prison for two long years.

"There will be an auction tonight where you and the other women and children will be sold to the highest bidders from mostly Asia. As part of the auction, my expectation is you will go for a high price.

"There will be no escape for you this time as the plan is for me to personally escort you to the shipping container that will take you and the rest of the merchandise to Asia."

Refusing to give Price more power over me, I bury the terror and fear. I stay silent.

"There will be no escape for you this time.

"If you survive the journey, you will be given to an evil man who will use you repeatedly. There will be no rescue as there will be no way to trace your disappearance.

"Now get up. I don't plan to spoil the merchandise before the auction and money changing hands."

Getting to my feet stiffly, I try hard not to shiver. Price grabs my arm hard enough to leave bruises and drags me through the door and down a large open space with cages lining the walls. Passing the cages of women and children, it's suddenly deathly silent. They are as terrified of Price as I am.

We reach a metal stairway that ascends obviously to the next floor.

At the top of the stairs is a door that opens to a glitzy stage with bright lights, speakers, and huge screens showing people of different nationalities and obviously from different places.

There is a platform where an auctioneer sits as they bring each woman or child up for sale. A young girl maybe seventeen is brought forward. The bidding is rapid and soon the girl is led way.

A child about seven years old is next, the greed and lust on the buyers' faces makes bile gather in the back of my throat.

Woman after woman, child after child is brought to the stage. They are beyond terrified and shivering in the bright lights. It makes me sick at heart and very afraid. I can't help the sudden wave of black despair that washes over me.

Then, it is my turn to stand on the stage. The roaring in my ears and tears in my eyes prevent me from clearly hearing the sick bidders' willingness to buy another human being. I feel humiliated with the sudden loss of my personhood, my humanity. These monsters are treating us like cattle. I feel the deluge as it sucks my hope and dreams down into an abyss. No hopes of rescue.

When I stumble off the stage, I am numb. Price grabs my arm in a tight grip and leads me back to the cage, I had been locked in before.

He follows me inside the cage, closing the door.

"You have much to make up to me Allory. As you have been sold, and the money is now being deposited into my account there is no need to keep you – the merchandise in pristine condition."

I watch him take out a pair of black leather gloves from his pocket. He points to the far wall of the cage and tells me to stand against it.

He walks closer to me and grabs my throat and squeezes until I can't breathe then releases me just before I lose consciousness. He does it repeatedly telling me if I fight him, he will suffocate me. I start to distance myself from the fear and the air hunger.

I am so much smaller in stature compared to his size and heavy muscles.

Price begins to beat me methodically, all the while avoiding my face. He pounds over my complete torso with specific attention to my ribs, with his huge, clenched fists. He turns me to face the cage wall with a hand on my shoulder to hold me up as he continues to beat me. When he releases me, I crumple to the floor whimpering in pain.

He again grabs me easily under one shoulder to hold me up while I stifle a scream. He turns me to face the cage wall and pummels my back, until I am gasping for air. I sink to the floor in torment. He pulls me up to pound my ribs again until I feel several give way. He grabs my right wrist and twists until it snaps. I scream in agony.

I barely register that he has undone his pants and is stroking himself.

Then he shoots his semen over my chest and stomach.

At that point I am losing consciousness. He throws me to the cement and kicks me a few more times. "I may have to reimburse the client for your fee if you arrive in less than pristine condition as I have a reputation to maintain."

Before he leaves, I hear him say I will never be able to escape with my injuries. His final threat sticks with me.

His last words, barely discernible through the pain "I will see you loaded into the container knowing the life you have is over. If you survive the journey to Asia, you will wish-- when you arrive-- that you died."

———◆———

Price sits in his office after he left Allory, he is regretting his loss of control. He is a businessman and knew that the merchandise needed to arrive in good condition.

He looks up the client and calls him to discuss the situation. He explains "the girl you purchased is no longer available. She escaped from one of my men and ran into the street. She was run over by a car and didn't survive. My man has been disciplined. I will refund your money. You will have first choice at a reduced price at next month's auction." His client is agreeable to the deal.

He hangs up satisfied that he hadn't tarnished his reputation. Allory likely was not going to survive the journey. He sent a message and a photo of Allory to their unloading crew in Asia to ensure she was dead when the container arrived. If she survived, his instructions were to kill her and dump the body.

I am barely aware when Price comes back with one of men who picks me up and throws me over his shoulder. The pain is excruciating, I lose consciousness again.

I barely rouse when they dump me in the back of panel truck crowded with other women and children. The back doors close and soon the truck is moving. All I can hear through the ravaging pain is the soft cries of children and sobs from women before I slip into unconsciousness again. I don't remember the rest of the trip, rousing only when the doors open with lights a distance away. Price kept his word to personally dump me in the container closing and locking the door.

Around me I faintly sense the women and children silent or sobbing. I fade away again, hoping I die before we reach our destination.

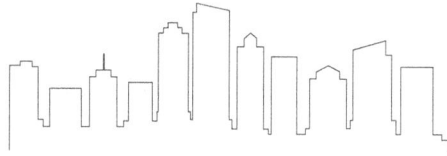

Chapter Forty

Connor and Sean both wanted to go to the docks with Marc and me. I explained that the situation is strictly a police matter now.

I give Angel an update to pass on to Allory's siblings.

"Tell them Allory is alive. We expect that Price will have her transported to the docks with the rest of the women and children sold at the auction."

I am about forty-five minutes behind Marc as I had to pick up my team along the way.

Marc and his Interpol team exit onto Central Street arriving at the southeast corner of the docks only entrance.

He provides his Port Authority security clearance dated for today to the armed guard at the gate. The guard had already been briefed to let Marc's and Jake's teams pass through the barricade, allowing them to intercept Price. The guard provides a map that identifies the location of Price's container before lifting the barricade.

Marc leaves one of his team to support the Port Authority guard.

Once through the entrance we continue to the northwest end of the facility where Price's container is located marked on the map. It is just after three am.

When Jake and his team arrive later, they go through the same security process that Marc's team had. Jake leaves Kyle with the one officer Marc had left to support the lone guard. They were hiding behind the gatehouse out of sight.

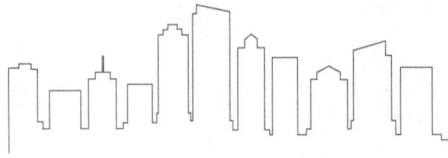

Chapter Forty-One

Jake's team hides two containers to the left side of Price's container while Marc's team hides two containers to the right on the ocean side of the docks. They wait for the panel truck with the women and children along with Price and his associates to arrive at the docks.

Sound carries easily this close to the water. The unmistakable sounds of gunshots echo in the direction of the dock entrance. Jake moves quickly to where Marc's team is hunkered down. It is now close to three fifteen in the morning.

Jake turns on his mic to talk to Kyle at the gate.

Kyle sounds a bit jacked up briefing Jake. "When the guard was explaining that the docks were closed tonight to clean up a hazardous spill from one of the containers. Price shot him and his truck plowed through the barricade followed by Price in his Ferrari.

"The guard was wearing a vest, but he was hit above the vest on his left side. I have called for an ambulance to arrive without siren or lights to get the guard to the hospital."

"We are going to have to ask for local RCMP support. I will let you know the details when we hear what that looks like," Jake says before keying off his mic.

Marc, Ric, and I talk, briefly. Price has shown he will use deadly force to get the women and children to the container.

Ric, the senior RCMP on the Interpol team agrees to call his boss in Ottawa with the time difference it is six am there. He reports that Price has shot the armed guard at the Port gate with the situation now likely deadly.

His boss puts him on hold as he calls the Deputy Commissioner in B.C. to ask for assistance.

The panel trunk arrives at the container followed by a red Ferrari. Three men get out of cab. Jake recognizes Price getting out of the sports car.

One man opens the container while another opens the doors to the panel truck.

The men have guns and prod the women and children to walk in single line to the container. It is apparent many of the women and children are in bad shape.

Price moves to stand at the right of the panel trunk. It appears he is waiting for someone. When no more women or children climb out of the panel truck that leaves only those too injured to walk without help.

His men jump up into the back of the truck to start taking the injured out and putting them in the container. There is no care taken with the injured, they are roughly dumped in the container.

After a look inside the panel truck, Price hops into the back, coming back with a woman in a blue pantsuit. When he gets close to the container Marc and Jake can see it is Allory. She appears unconscious. Price carries Allory to the container and drops her inside like a piece of garbage. All the cargo is now loaded because he closes and locks the container door.

Jake flinches watching the callous treatment of the women and children by Price and his men. To wait without intervening was torture, particularly seeing him, callously dump Allory inside the container. His satisfied smile as he closed and locked the container incites Jake to violence. He can barely hold himself back.

Ric's boss from Ottawa calls him back as the container is loaded and locked.

He quickly relays to us that the Deputy Commissioner is on his way to take control of the situation. He has called in the local Critical Incident and Hostage Negotiation teams which are currently enroute.

Now the container is loaded, Jake and Marc step away from their teams knowing that the container is not going anywhere as the container ship that Price had planned to use to get the women and children to Asia has been impounded by the Port Authority.

"We can't let Price, and his men leave the docks," Jake insists

"I will have Ric call out to Price to make him aware we are here. If you alert Kyle and my guy at the gate, that we will try to prevent Price from leaving."

Jake turns on his team mic. "Jensen are you and Eric still close to the Port Gate?"

"Yes, we are just a half a block from the gate. I expect Kyle and Marc's man may need back up should Price and his associates try to escape the docks. Has the container been loaded?" he asks.

"Yes, we will have to challenge Price to keep him at the container until the local RCMP teams arrive to help us with the situation. Keep me posted of any problems," Jake whispers into his mic. Jensen responds affirmatively.

Jake waves Marc over. stepping close to whisper in his ear. "Do we have ETA for the Deputy Commissioner and RCMP teams?

"Should be within the next thirty minutes," whispers Marc.

Jake turns his mic on. "Jensen status report," he says in a low voice.

"Eric and I are at the gate. The guard is enroute to hospital."

Jake tells him that the Deputy Commissioner for the RCMP in BC will be arriving with the Critical Incident and Hostage Negotiation Teams in the next half hour. "Keep me updated," he says keying off his mic.

Marc leans close. "Ric is going to confront Price now," he warns in a whisper.

Ric calls out, "Price this is the RCMP you are under arrest for human trafficking. Surrender your weapons."

"Never I don't plan on going back to prison," he yells jumping behind the back side of the container while firing a shot toward where he thinks Ric is.

All of Price's men scatter drawing their weapons to shoot into the darkness. Marc's team shoots back hitting several men before they could take cover behind their truck or other containers.

Jensen alerts Jake. "The Deputy Commissioner is at the gate with the Critical Incident and Hostage Negotiation teams having arrived without sirens.

"I gave them a map lying on the guard's desk showing where Price's container is. "They are coming to your location from the far left of your position to the end of the dock then make their way to you. They should be there soon."

"Message received," whispers Jake.

Ric and Marc are relieved the local support has arrived as they are now in a standoff with injured women and children that need medical assistance quickly and Price's men taking gunfire.

As they wait tensely, Ric tells me and Jake he worries about the timing of the standoff with Price, delaying the rendering of medical assessment and care to the badly injured women and children in the container.

Ric fills us in about the bureaucracy as we wait, "The Deputy Commissioner will be responsible to contact Family Services and The Office to Combat Trafficking in Persons as their mandate is human rights specifically those of the victims of trafficking to provide support and reconnect these women and children with their families or help relocate to a safe place.

"We need to resolve the standoff and provide medical care for the women and children first."

Marc's relieved local support is available for the women and children.

Price and his colleagues have been quiet for the last while.

There are hundreds of containers around the docks and equipment to hide behind. There is only one entry and exit from the docks aside from the water side. It is not a viable escape for Price and his associates because all boats along the docks have been locked down by the Port Authority in anticipation of Price choosing that route.

Marc reflects on his original contact with the Port Authority Vice president and chief human resource officer when his team came to them with the allegations of human trafficking through the Port of Vancouver. She and the executive team have been behind us from the start.

It took a full day of reviewing webcam footage to identify Price's associates that were accessing the terminal. We suspected Price had an employee at the Terminal who sponsored them on their application for a pass, that likely went through a local trucking company that moves containers.

It explained how Price and his associates could come and go from docks. The Port Authority has moved quickly to identify those associates.

I turn on my mic to connect with Jake.

"Does any of your team have eyes on Price and his associates? He and his men have gone silent since Ric called out to him."

"No," Jake replies.

"There isn't much our teams can do before the reinforcements arrive. The Emergency Response and Crisis Negotiation Teams are needed to secure the area and begin dialogue with Price to render help to his men and the women and children in the container."

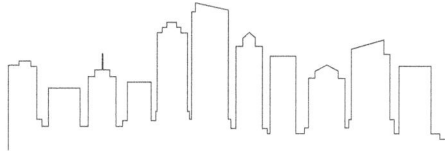

Chapter Forty-Two

The Deputy Commissioner with two RCMP teams and four First Responders with emergency supplies come in silently on foot from the far-left side of the dock and then negotiated between the containers to where the map showed the location of Price's container. Jake was apprised by Kyle they left their vehicles with two ambulances close to Jake and Marc's teams located at the gate.

Me and Marc's teams move silently toward them while the darkness of night is fading.

The commissioner is a tall man with dark hair. He eludes calm and competence. He introduces Chris the team leader for the Crisis Negotiator Team and Trevor the team leader for Emergency Response Team. Both teams have two-way intercom to allow for continuous communication between the teams and both leaders.

Marc introduces his Interpol team then Jake and his team.

"I was thoroughly briefed of the situation from Ric's superior" explains the Commissioner. "I would like to turn this situation over to Chris and Trevor.

"Our priority is beginning negotiation with Price to release the women and children. I understand that many are in bad shape. I had an update regarding the Port Authority guard. He is currently in surgery," adds the Commissioner.

"We have heard nothing from Price and his associates in the last twenty minutes. "They scattered when we made Price aware we were here. Price told us he has no plans to return to prison," Ric briefs the local RCMP teams.

Chris explains. "I will try to open dialogue with Price while Trevor's team spreads out in fading night to pinpoint the location of Price and his men.

"It is close to four am with urgency to find where Price and his men are hiding."

Chris has a colleague pass him a megaphone. "Leon Price my name is Chris with the RCMP. I am hoping we can work out how to de-escalate this situation without further harm done on either side," he says calmly.

Out of the darkness Price yells back. "I want me and my men to be able to leave the docks unimpeded."

"We need to talk about the women and children in the locked container first. I understand there are many that need medical attention. You need to release them first, for first responders to assess them and transport those needing medical care," replies Chris firmly.

"Are any of your associates injured?" he asks Price.

"Yes, one has a belly wound, another has a leg injury, and one was hit in the back," he responds back.

Meanwhile, Trevor's team spreads out quickly to make the most of the darkness before early morning light makes the situation more dangerous for everyone; his men constantly checking in.

"We have located three men hiding behind a container down to the left side of the dock says one officer. "It looks like all three are injured," he reports to Trevor.

"We see another man on the far side of the container that holds the women and children, I think it might be Price," responds another officer.

"I want you three to keep Price and his men in sight. While I talk with Chris to see if he can negotiate with Price to treat his men for releasing the women and children needing medical assistance now," Trevor instructs his men.

Trevor turns to Chris. "Can you see if Price will trade medical treatment for his men in turn for the release of the women and children in the container or at the very least have those women and children who are seriously injured released."

The Commissioner interrupts," I have called BC ambulance with a request for four units of first responders to provide us support for both Price's men as well as the women and children. They will wait at the entrance gate until it is safe to come in. I understand from Jake and Marc they have men at the gate to stop unauthorized entry."

Chris calls out to Price. "Would you trade treatment for your men for release of some of the women and children," he asks Price.

"I want my guys treated but no release of the women and children. They are my only bargaining chip. Do you think I am stupid," Price hollers back.

"Ok," says Chris. "What if you just let us in the container to get the women and children with the worse injuries?"

"I will consider it. First treat and stabilize my injured men," he shouts back.

"They will have to first lay down their weapons and kick them out of reach before I will allow the first responder to treat them," dictates Chris.

"Kick away your weapons men so you can be treated. You are no use to me wounded or dead," instructs Price to his men trapped behind the container to the left side of the dock.

Meanwhile, Trevor's men have their scopes on the three injured men seeing them kick away their weapons away as instructed with the rattle of the guns heard hitting the dock.

Chris turns to Trevor. "We need three first responders to pair with three officers to treat Price's men'.

Chris lowers his voice to a whisper, asking Trevor to have one of his sharp shooters keep his scope on Price constantly. He believes Price will move soon as the left side of container where the women and children are leaves him too open.

The sky is lightening when the three first responders with their officer companions work their way to Price's injured men. The officers pick up abandoned weapons and unload the ammunition along the way.

One officer frisks the injured men for hidden weapons before the first responder initiates assessment and treatment.

Chris calls out to Price. "Your men need transport to hospital."

"No transport," orders Price. "Just patch them up!"

Trevor checks in with the officer following Price's movements. He is now one container down to the right from his previous position.

"We have treated your men. Now let's talk about the most seriously injured women and children in the container that need treatment. If you refuse treatment for them things are going to get very tough for you.

"There is only one exit from this dock, and it is covered by my team. There is no chance of escape. So, what are you going to do now Price?" Chris asks.

There was silence as Chris waits for Price's response.

"Let us help the women and children." Chris repeats. "If you won't let us open the container. You do it," he demands of Price.

"What do I get if I open the container," challenges Price.

"It means you are willing to work on this situation to resolve without more bloodshed," answers Chris.

"Ok, so what do I get in return," Price demands.

"We continue our dialogue to reach a settlement to the situation here without anyone else getting hurt," replies Chris.

Price has been steadily moving back to the container where the women and children are. He cautiously creeps around to the door, lifting the lever one- handed, gun in the other while he slides the door open wide enough to slip inside the container. He comes out with a little girl of about eight with his hand around her throat and gun to her head.

"What are you going to negotiate now," he taunts Chris.

Two snipers are locked on Price's position. Suddenly he turns to move to a new position using the child as a shield. He sees two officers. He starts to fire on them when he is hit in the upper left shoulder by the sniper that has been following him. He loses his grip on the little girl.

One of the officers grabs her to get her to safety while the other relieves Price of his weapon.

Trevor calls for the ambulances at the entrance.

One of the first responders' who treated Price's men runs over to assess his injuries.

He tries to slow the bleeding from the bullet that went through the left upper shoulder very close to his heart and other internal organs.

The ambulances with paramedics start arriving a few minutes later.

The herculin task now, is to triage all the wounded including Price, his men and all the women and children from the container. Determining with each of the wounded what level of care they require.

Trevor's team has officers with Price and his men for security purposes.

Running to the container, Jake opens both doors wide to let the women and children out. He desperately searches for Allory as women and children slowly crawl outside.

After a few minutes, only the women who are injured and unable to move on their own are left in the container. Two paramedics enter the container to assess their injuries.

That is when Jake finds Allory. She is lying face down and not moving.

He is afraid to move her. Kneeling to check her pulse, it is steady but slow. He gently turns her onto her back, and she moans softly. She cradles her right wrist to chest, and she seems to be breathing very shallowly. Jake hazards a guess that Price likely fractured ribs and her wrist.

Allory and the other injured women and children not able to walk are put on stretchers after being triaged by the paramedics, who determined their medical needs.

Allory is prioritized to one of the first arriving ambulances, ironically so was Price.

Once Allory is safely in the back of the ambulance, Jake calls Connor.

"She is alive and being transported to hospital. From what I can gather so far, she has been badly beaten by Price. They are taking her to St. Paul's Hospital. I will meet you there as I will go with her in the ambulance."

Scanning the crowd Jake sees Marc. talking with Chris and Trevor, I walk over to let him know where Allory is. He takes off running when I point out the ambulance. I follow slowly feeling like hundred years old.

I stop to talk with Ric, Marc's team leader and the Deputy Commissioner who has called in services tailored to help the women and children exposed to human trafficking. He will determine if more paramedics are needed to assess medical issues with the women and children from the container, now sitting huddled with blankets on the dock.

The hard work of this night is just starting but more help is on the way.

All the women and children will have medical evaluation and care based on the extent of their injuries.

Ric agrees to manage the situation with the other RCMP teams and the Commissioner. He and the rest of our teams will assist with mop up. Ric will attend briefings for both me and Marc with the local RCMP teams later in the day.

I key my mic to Kyle at the gate with a brief update. I ask that he and the rest of Marc and I's teams at the gate render assistance. I ask him to check in with Ric who is our designated liaison for our teams on the dock.

When Allory is ready for transport, Marc gets in the back, and I ride shotgun with the driver.

I call Angel to briefly update her and ask her to drive Connor, Sean and Avery to St. Paul's Hospital."

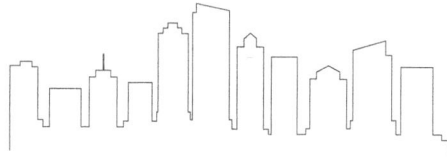

Chapter Forty-Three

Marc sits in the back of the ambulance with his hand in Allory's. Her beautiful face is unmarred, but he knows that her body is another story altogether.

What other horrors has she suffered at the hands of Price.

If he wasn't already almost dead, He would kill him over and over for what he has done to Allory.

Just as he was contemplating Price's demise, they enter the emergency bay at the hospital and emergency staff are opening the back. He jumps out and stays out of the way although he wants to be right by her side.

Jake stands shoulder to shoulder with him as Allory is taken into emergency. The first responder takes pity on us and leads us to the waiting area where we spot Sean, Connor, and Avery.

They are pale and shaking when we reach them.

"Marc, what do you know?" Connor asks hoarsely.

"Not much, besides she is unconscious. We are pretty sure she has been badly beaten. She likely has a fractured wrist and ribs. She didn't regain consciousness during transport."

Avery draws in a deep breath, stricken. Sean is silent. Connor looks sad and guilt -ridden.

I remind them, "Allory is strong; she will pull through, but she is going to need all of us."

Grabbing chairs, Jake and I sit with the siblings in the waiting room.

After two hours a female emergency physician comes to give us an update.

"Allory has a compound fracture of her right wrist. She has three broken ribs on her right side. She has multiple large contusions over her torso consistent with a brutal beating. Her fractured ribs and likely rough treatment resulted in internal injuries. She is currently in surgery to stop the bleeding.

"We found semen on her clothes, but no evidence of sexual assault or penetration."

Avery starts to cry. Connor puts his arm around her and holds her tight.

Sean wordless is clenching his jaw.

Marc looks at the doctor and asks the important question. "Is Allory going to be alright?"

The doctor looks at each of them. "She's holding her own. Once she is

moved to the ward, you will be able to see her. The surgeon will come to update you on her condition.

"Due to the circumstances of her injuries, I have recommended family be able to stay with her around the clock."

After the physician leaves, Sean gets up to pace. Avery pulls herself together.

We wait for three hours before we hear any news.

A nurse kindly comes to update us. "Allory has been transferred upstairs.

"She is in stable condition but remains unconscious." We all breathe a sigh of relief.

Riding the elevator, we get off at the fourth floor. Allory is in the second room on the right. We have decided that one of us would stay with her around the clock. Pulling a chair close to the bed, Avery takes Allory's left hand in hers.

The female surgeon briefly comes to talk to us an hour later.

"The beating, fractured ribs and any movement after that caused internal bleeding. She reassured us they repaired the damage.

"Her fractured wrist has been set and casted. She will need physiotherapy support for the ribs and wrist after the cast is removed.

"I will be in to check on her tomorrow," she tells us before she leaves.

The next morning, I talk with the doctor about Allory's condition as she has not woken up yet. She reminds me her injuries were serious.

Overall, the physician felt Allory was young and strong and likely to regain consciousness soon.

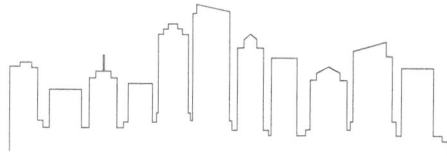

Chapter Forty-Four

Over the next forty-eight hours Allory is unconscious, it is difficult for each of us.

Taking it the hardest, Sean remains present but very angry.

In contrast Avery just sits holding Allory's hand until I talk her into sleeping on the sofa bed we brought into Allory's private room.

Marc is never far from her and sits talking to her softly in French when we need a rest.

He attends virtual meetings with his Interpol team in the waiting room down the hall. They are shifting through all the evidence against Price's men that survived to ensure they are charged with trafficking.

Avery called her friend Céline who flew in the first day when Allory was still unconscious. She couldn't stay longer. She asked that Avery keep her up to date before she left.

Drowsing in the chair next to her bed when she opens her eyes in the late afternoon with a soft groan.

"Hi," I say gently holding her left hand in mine.

She looks at me in confusion, her gaze hazy. "Where am I Connor?" she asks in a raspy voice.

I grab a glass of water on the bedside table and assist her to drink slowly through the straw before answering her.

"You are in the hospital. What do you remember?"

She looks away before answering. "Bits and pieces".

I push the call button to alert the nurse who will have her physician come assess her now Allory is awake.

The nurse arrives and checks the monitors. She asks Allory a few questions and then tells me she would let her physician know she is awake.

"Where is everyone?" Allory asks.

"They went to shower, change, and eat something. We have all been keeping a close watch over you since you were admitted two nights ago."

Allory is quiet for a few moments. "I remember being at the warehouse, the auction and the beating after.

"Connor, I think I am broken inside and out," she tells me as tears run down her cheeks.

It wrecks me that she is so badly hurt and for a moment I don't know what to say. I brush the tears gently off her cheeks.

"We are all here for you Allory! We will help in any way to get you better and whole again."

Before I can continue, the physician walks into the room. Dr. Martin is tall with long black hair and has a caring and kind demeanor as she talks to Allory.

"You have several injuries we need to talk about, after I re-examine you. I was a bit concerned that it has taken awhile for you to regain consciousness," she says, as she pulls the curtain, and I step back.

Once the exam is complete the physician takes a seat across the bed from me.

"Allory, you have three fractured ribs, a compound fracture of your right wrist and multiple large contusions and swelling from the beating, and the rough treatment you received. You had internal bleeding we repaired in the operating room."

Feeling overwhelmed with the doctor's description of her injuries, her gaze is stuck to Connor's face.

Dr Martin continues. "I would like to repeat abdominal imaging both an ultrasound and x-ray to ensure there are no lingering complications which will slow your recovery. If you continue to improve, I will discharge you home in one or two days.

"Do you have any questions Allory?"

"Then I can hope for a full recovery?" she asks the doctor.

"Yes, if you continue to progress you will make a slow but full recovery," confirms Dr. Martin. "The repeat ultrasound is to check the operative repair.

"I work in private practice so once you are discharged, I will follow up with you in the community to ensure your recovery goes well.

"Additionally, I contacted a trauma counselor who will visit with you prior to discharge and continue to follow you in the community.

"I understand from your family this is not your first trauma although I hear that you are a strong and resilient woman. There are times when all of us need support, and I think this situation warrants that.

"I will leave you with Connor and check in with you tomorrow," she says as she leaves the room.

During the physician visit I text Sean, Avery, and Marc to let them know Allory is awake.

Turning my focus back to Allory her eyes are closed; I know she isn't asleep because her breathing is ragged. I reach over and put my hand over her ice cold one.

"Allory, Price was shot at the docks, and he subsequently died from his injury during surgery. His associates are in jail. It is over. You're safe," I reinforce in a calm firm voice.

Allory doesn't open her eyes, but tears track down her face. Snatching a Kleenex from the bedside table, I gently soak up her tears.

"I hate that he hurt you so badly. I never wanted it to go that way. I blame myself for not finding another solution," I whisper.

Allory opens her eyes. "No Connor. This was my choice. You can't blame yourself. There really was no other way."

Before we can have further conversation, the porter comes to take her to the imaging department. It was very hard to let go of her hand, because she watches me like I am her lifeline until her bed disappears down the hall.

I text Marc, Avery, and Sean, updating then that she is awake and down at the imaging department.

Marc arrives first, followed by Avery and Sean.

I explain the details of her doctor visit and next steps stressing that Allory will get better.

The waiting is brutal for all of us. Allory left nearly an hour ago.

She returns to the room a few minutes later.

Sitting next to the bedside, Avery gently takes her left hand. The rest of us stand in a circle around her bed. Elated Allory is awake and back with us.

Dr. Martin returns an hour later to give us the good news, The new imaging found no further issues in her abdomen including no further bleeding and the ribs are stable.

The doctor tells us if she continues to improve, she will likely be discharged as early as tomorrow afternoon.

When Dr. Martin leaves, I follow her outside the room.

I ask her questions about how to ensure a successful discharge home.

"Allory will be referred to home nursing care, they will recommend equipment and supports for Allory to recover at home. She will have a follow up appointment in two weeks to see me in the community."

Making a call to my office to ensure there were no outstanding issues, I return to her room. I see Allory has fallen asleep in the meantime.

"I'm going home to nap, shower and returning later in the evening," Our plan since Allory was admitted was to rotate one of us with her continuously until she is discharged.

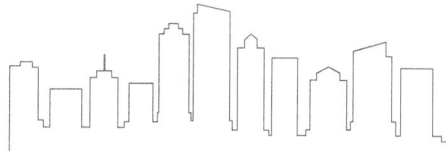

Chapter Forty-Five

Sean looks at his baby sister asleep in her hospital bed. A rage breaks loose inside him when he thinks about how that monster hurt her again. The only bright spot in this whole mess is the bastard is dead.

Sean looks at Avery nodding his head at the door. We leave Allory with Marc.

"I need to check my work sites. I will bring food when I come back. I shouldn't be more than a few hours.

"Are you staying Avery?"

"Yes, I plan to stay until Connor comes back. Then I will go home for a rest.

"I admit I am not quite back to my old self since the car accident."

Sean understands why Marc was not leaving, still one of us should also be here.

Getting in his truck, Sean heads to his worksite that had the suspicious fire. He suspects Price was involved; he just couldn't prove it.

Opening the door to the work site trailer, he spies his site supervisor behind his desk.

"Hi Glen, any news from the Fire Marshal or WorkSafe?"

"No, but that doesn't surprise me, 'government bureaucracy' grinds slowly."

"There has been no suspicious activity noted by night security.

"The crew is more vigilant during work hours," Glen explains.

"The fire puts us behind in the construction despite moving funds to accommodate the delay. Let's just take one day at a time for now. Talk to you tomorrow."

Driving across town to another of his building sites, this one nearing completion. He has a brief chat with the crew.

Taking a phone call from the foreman for the third work site. Making a trip to the site unnecessary today.

Running by his condo, Sean showers and changes. He is more settled now that Allory is awake.

Stopping by a nearby market, to buy hot meals to go, he grabs water and pop to take back to the hospital. Sean needs to ensure his family is fed.

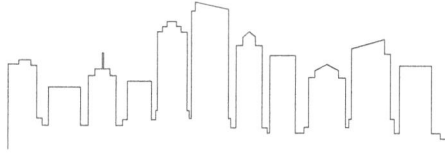

Chapter Forty-Six

Avery feels a profound sense of relief knowing Price died in surgery because he can't ever touch Allory again.

Now more than ever we need to support each other and give Allory the time to work through this new trauma.

Slipping silently into Allory's room, Seeing Marc. The way he looks at Allory sleeping, melts some of the coldness inside me.

Knowing that look, my heart settles. This fine man loves my baby sister. Believing that will make a difference in the end. I sit down on the other side of the bed and gently hold Allory's hand in mine.

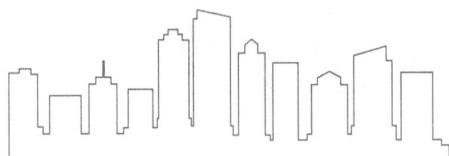

Chapter Forty-Seven

I am in the hospital for two days before they discharge me.

We, including Marc return to the condo because it can accommodate all of us.

My worried and angry siblings aren't allowing me out of their sight. I know I gave them a terrible fright.

But in my mind, being the bait was worth it because I have my life back.

I know Price wanted me dead, but I was just too stubborn to die. My freedom for the brutal beating and injuries I sustained doesn't balance the scales. All the negative thoughts I wrestled with after my rape and first abduction are back.

The therapist Dr. Martin recommended does house calls. She has come to have several sessions with me in the last week. I know I am messed up. The nightmares are brutal with sleep patchy at night.

I am trying to bring these difficult dreams into daylight and don't suffer in silence anymore.

When it is a tough day, I allow my feelings to come out instead of holding them in.

I'm relearning how to focus on what I can control, and I lean on my family and Marc when needed.

Most importantly, I tap into self-compassion.

I am working on triggers that exploit my fears.

Understanding most days this will be a journey for me. I can't just fix me that easily because the memories of the trauma will linger inside me. For now, I take one day and one negative feeling at a time.

Avery and Marc have been my touch stones. Sean comes and plays with me, and Connor is a quiet presence just there when I need to lean on him.

The glimmer of a potential future is a dream worth chasing. As I heal, I am proud I survived the Monster. I lived and he died. That is not charitable, but he was an evil man who did really bad things. I have no remorse that he is likely rotting in hell where he deserves to be.

I am not ready to talk with my family about the auction at the warehouse. That topic I leave strictly with my therapist.

Price selling me at the auction like a commodity for money was dehumanizing. He took the value of my personhood ripping it away from me. I am working every day to understand and assimilate this new trauma.

Forgetting the other women and children who had been in the container with me bound for Asia and Hell, is impossible.

Wanting to help in some way, Connor and I are exploring with the Office to Combat Trafficking how I may help woman and children rescued from traffickers.

I also talked with Jake about Price's human trafficking ring. He told me everyone involved was arrested and his whole operation shut down.

And finally, I have time to explore a relationship with Marc. That beautiful man has stayed with me since my discharge from hospital last week. He has seen me at my worst after Price brutalized me.

He doesn't allow me to shirk support or caring while I learn again to find the strong woman inside me who is a survivor.

He ensures I don't miss therapy appointments and takes me out of my head when I am stuck there.

My wrist is still in a cast, and I will need physical therapy when the cast comes off. My ribs still give me pain if I move too quickly, but my doctor tells me they are healing slowly. I hope to get into pool therapy and work on my physical fitness after my cast is removed.

Avery has recovered mostly from her car accident and her GP tells her the fatigue will lessen over time.

She continues to be my closest confidant when the bad memories surface.

I can't believe that Céline flew to see me when I was in the hospital but that was in the first two days when I was unconscious. I love her for coming all that way. I try to call or text her most days since I left the hospital.

Continuing in his big brother role, Connor reminds me every day to take time to heal. Work, friends, and life decisions can wait until I am whole again.

I just need a strategy to help my brothers deal with what happened to me. They are so angry and feeling guilty about what happened. How do I absolve them of these destructive feelings? I will recruit Avery to help me with that.

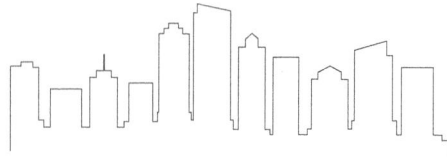

Chapter Forty-Eight

The next morning at breakfast with Marc, we discuss his plans with Interpol and Jake's offer of partnership in his company. While I share an earlier conversation this morning with my boss Andre about the UBC partnership.

I get up to start clearing the table. I smile when Marc starts to help. I give him the look he is now well acquainted with.

"Let's talk about what you and I's future could look like," I ask.

"As you know Allory, I've taken a month's leave from Interpol to seriously consider joining Jake's company as a partner to lead the expansion in Marseille."

I weigh in on his plans for work. "I don't think you could find a better partner than Jake. He has built a great team with a stellar reputation.

"You would be working with your best friend which is a bonus.

"You also know that I want to return to France, but I am open to having a home here too."

Recalling, my earlier conversation with my boss, he has given me latitude with deadlines for my remote work and the UBC partnership.

"Andre has been pleased with all my work and asked for me to check in with him weekly, now."

Marc nods with approval knowing I struggled with how much to tell my boss.

"Let's take each day as it comes Allory. We have already made the important decision to be in a relationship and make it a priority for both of us."

"Is it okay if I invite Sean for dinner tonight. I think he is struggling."

Texting Sean about dinner, he responds right away asking what he can bring. Replying, I tell him bring a bottle of wine.

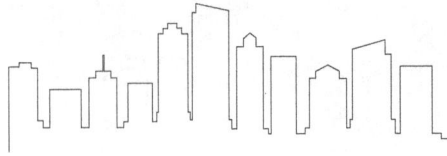

Chapter Forty-Nine

Arriving at six o'clock, Sean hands me a nice Merlot for dinner. He comments on how I am moving easier and have more colour in my cheeks.

Watching Sean talk to Marc about his building projects, he is just not himself. He is quieter and I can see shadows in his eyes even when he smiles. I know Avery and Connor are worried about Sean too.

Usually, he is always an upbeat guy, I am not sure I want to ruin dinner by asking. Instead, I lean into him on the sofa after dinner. Teasing him and laughing at his silly jokes.

When Sean leaves, I give him a tight hug holding him for a moment before he leaves in the elevator.

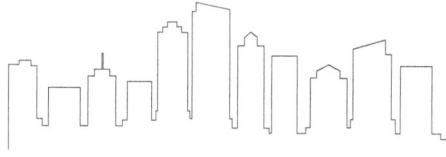

Chapter Fifty

Sitting in his office in the evening almost two weeks since Allory was discharged from the hospital, Jake is exhausted.

Closing his eyes, he asks himself if there is anything else he could have done to change the outcome for Allory. He wonders if Connor feels the same way.

He picks up his cell phone and dials Connor's number. He answers straight away.

"Can you talk now?"

"Yes, I am in my office catching up on paperwork."

"I need to talk to someone who can relate to the guilt I have about Allory's injuries from Price. The memory wrecks me."

There was silence as Connor thought that over.

"It wrecks me too," admits Connor.

"We did have a plan to eliminate him. I still wonder if we shouldn't have," Jake says in a low voice.

"I would be lying if I said I didn't agree with you," Connor sighs deeply.

"But it would have been a whole lot more complicated since Interpol and RCMP were involved. And if we got caught and sent to prison, it would be hard to explain to my sisters. If you were asking Sean though, he would agree with the idea of ending Price before he hurt Allory again.

"At the end of the day, Jake, we are not murderers, and I believe if we had killed Price, we would have been changed in a way that we could never come back from. Crossing legal moral lines isn't what the good guys do."

"You're right, but it is difficult living with the consequences of what Price did to Allory, knowing we ethically couldn't simply make him disappear."

"To change the subject, how close are you to convincing Marc to become your partner and lead the Marseille operation?"

"Marc has taken a leave from Interpol as I am pretty sure he is going join me."

"I would be happy to come on board as a silent partner. I am bored with my practice and looking for new challenges."

"Let me set up a meeting with the three of us. Text me your availability and I will organize a date and time," Jake ends the call.

Mulling over Connor's offer, Jake is sure he would be a good fit with him and Marc.

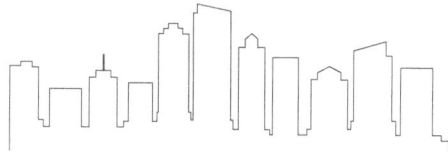

Chapter Fifty-One

Sean is finished up at the Westside building project for today and goes home to shower and change.

Texting Avery and Connor to see if they will meet him at his place. He offers to cook which increases the chance that both will show up.

Connor and Avery text back telling him they would be over in an hour leaving time for him to walk to the market to purchase produce and salmon fillets for dinner.

Loving his neighbourhood, because everything is within walking distance from his condo.

He makes a Cobb salad, basmati rice and a special sauce made of butter, lemon, light cream, and Parmesan cheese to bake the salmon fillets in. He's opening a Sauvignon Blanc to have with dinner when the buzzer rings.

He lets his siblings into the building and unlocks his door for them.

They walk through the entryway when he is pouring the wine.

Avery gives Sean a white box. "Who has time to bake?" she asks while grabbing a seat next to Connor, across the counter from Sean.

"It was nice to be invited to dinner," says Connor.

Sean takes a deep breath. "Just let me get this off my chest. The rage has had a firm grip on my emotions since Price brutalized Allory again."

"Finally," Avery sighs. "We have been worried because you are so angry Sean."

Connor gives me an understanding look. "Each of us is grappling with deep anger after what Price did to Allory, Sean."

"Now she is back at the condo, the rage in me is still there boiling below the surface. My deepest regret is that we couldn't find another way to get rid of Price.

"I know we couldn't put a hit out on him," he jokes. "That would make us criminals like him."

"Being the joker in the family, there is nowhere to put the rage."

"Would you be willing to talk with a counselor?" asks Avery.

"I've been talking with a counselor," Connor admits.

"The problems started with sleep, then difficulties concentrating at work."

Sean is surprised to hear his brother is talking to a counselor.

"Is it helping?" he asks.

"It is slow going, hate feeling vulnerable, but having such guilt for allowing Allory to be hurt and the flashbacks from my near brush with death were driving me nuts.

"Being the oldest, regretting not doing a better job taking care of her and the situation."

"Connor, come on," bursts out Avery.

"Allory needed an ending." she argues passionately.

"Let me remind you he targeted us as well even before he was paroled."

"We need to be talking about the harm he has done to us as well as Allory."

"Don't think she doesn't have guilt about my car accident, your fire Sean and Connor's near miss. Because she does!"

Listening to his sister, Sean puts the prepared salmon into the oven to bake for twenty minutes. He refills their wine glasses before moving them to more comfortable seating on his divan.

"Glad you both came tonight. It helps to put things in perspective."

"We experienced a terrible trauma seeing Allory injured and all of us have a sense of responsibility for what happened," explains Avery.

"And you're right Avery, Allory needed a finite closure to Price. And we all needed to give her an opportunity for a life no longer endangered by that man," says Sean.

Avery pauses to look at the painting he has on the far wall. "Where did you get that painting. It is exquisite."

"Found it in an out of the way gallery in North Vancouver. It suits my place." He is pleased she noticed.

"This rage inside me stems from not being able to protect Allory the first, second or third time from Price's brutality.

"Even when Price came after us three it was scary but not surprising as he was targeting us to further terrorize Allory.

"Avery, your suggestion to work with a counselor is a good idea. Being present for Allory and both of you is important to me. Learning new ways to deal with my rage will be a relief!"

"Sean, I just texted you names of good counselors. The best way is to look up their ratings and reviews then choose one based on a trial session. Personal fit should be the primary consideration."

"Thanks Avery, I will review the list and book an initial appointment soon."

The timer on the stove goes off. We move to the kitchen. Setting out plates and utensils after taking out the salmon from the oven and rice from the stove. Avery uncovers the salad after I take it from the fridge.

We take turns filling our plates. Sean refills the wine glasses. We are quiet with the first bites of food.

"As usual dinner is superb," exclaims Avery.

While eating the delicious strawberry short cake dessert, Connor gets a serious look on his face.

"Lately my law practice has been less challenging and interesting. A change may help me to be more engaged.

'You both know Jake has asked Marc to go into partnership with him.

"Talking with Jake last night, he may be interested in a silent partner who could be counsel for both Vancouver and Marseille who could qualify to practice in France."

Laughing Sean ribs his brother. "Wondering when you were going to admit you are bored. Investing the remainder of the trust fund with them is great."

"You haven't been happy for a while Connor. New challenges may be just the thing to get you excited and engaged again," adds Avery.

"When Allory gets better, she wants to return to Marseille.

"The four of us should consider options to maintain closer ties," suggests Avery.

"Avery thanks for the list of counsellors," says Sean.

"It will be great to learn how to manage my rage and learn new ways to handle my emotions."

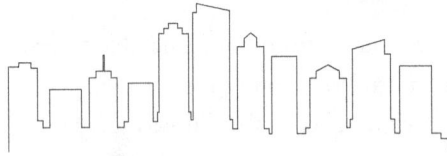

Chapter Fifty-Two

It is now six weeks into my recovery. I am more mobile since starting pool therapy. I was so happy to get that heavy, ugly cast off my arm.

My nightmares are improving, and I am feeling stronger every day.

I have resumed my remote work for the museum.

I order dinner from a local restaurant to arrive in two hours as I was busy with my in-person and virtual meetings this afternoon.

I have a shower dry and flat iron my hair, applying light make up before donning a simple green dress that buttons in the front with lower heeled black shoes.

Then I go looking for Marc.

I find him in the small study down the hall on the computer. He looks up when he notices me standing quietly in the doorway.

"Hey beautiful, love the dress. What is the occasion?"

"I just wanted to dress nice as I will be meeting your parents for the first time.

"I've ordered in dinner before we have the video call with your parents."

"Do I need to change?"

"No, you are perfect," I say quietly.

"I thought we could sit in the living room and admire the view of the harbour."

Once we are settled on the sofa, I take off my shoes and curl up next to Marc. We are quiet for several moments, then we both speak at once.

"You go first," Allory laughs.

"You are looking much better over the last few days. I admire how you are working hard to get better with support from physio and therapist."

Allory smiles. "Your support makes this easier for me. I know life is precious.

"I love you. I think you are amazing, and everything I would want in a man. I am not sure things are going to be easy for us because of the things Price did to me. But if you can be patient with me, I want to be with you in every way."

"Allory. I will wait for as long as you need to make this relationship work."

"Would you like a glass of wine, Marc?"

"That would be great,"

"I opened the wine earlier, it's been breathing," she tells me coming back with two glasses. Allory sighs, taking her first sip.

"Connor is going to join the partnership with Jake and me, focusing on providing legal services.

"Jake is arranging a meeting with the three of us to discuss plans further. What do you think?"

I pause as I take in everything Marc said.

"Wow! I am glad that Connor wants to partner with you and Jake. He needs a change."

"I see a future where both of us will come and go between Vancouver and Marseille."

The lobby phone starts to ring.

"That's dinner arriving," I jump up to answer the phone.

"I will go get the delivery," Marc says heading to the elevator.

Soon we are at the dining table eating a delicious meal.

We take our second glasses of wine to sit in the living room.

Marc goes to get his laptop so he can have the video call he arranged with his parents. I sit next to him as this will be the first time I will meet them. I am a bit nervous to make a good impression.

He initiates the video link.

I see a man who looks remarkably like Marc on the screen. Sitting next to him, is a beautiful older woman. I note Marc has her eyes.

Marc introduces me to his parents. "We are very happy to meet you Allory, his mom tells me graciously. "Marc has told us all about this amazing woman he has met."

Marc dives into the purpose of the call. His parents listen carefully as he describes the partnership with Jake.

It is obvious that they know Jake well. They go over the pros and cons and conclude this is a very good venture.

"I will apprise Jake of my decision to be his partner and begin my resignation from Interpol. Thanks for all your support."

The call ends with his parents hoping that they will see us soon.

Marc closes the computer and sets it on the side table next to him.

We cuddle on the sofa after the video call.

There are kisses and gentle petting, but I realize for the first time I want more.

Later he walks me to the door of my bedroom. I hug him tightly. He kisses me goodnight.

I get ready for bed, leaving a small night light shining near the desk, so I am never in full darkness.

As I slip into sleep, I think about Marc's sweet kisses tonight.

———❖———

Marc has a hard time getting to sleep after he walks Allory to her bedroom. He left his door ajar in case she wakes in the night.

Looking at the bedside clock it is now past midnight.

Determinedly he closes his eyes and takes slow breaths. At the edge of sleep, He hears Allory call out.

He jumps out of bed and rushes into her room, pausing he realizes he needs to approach her slowly.

She is strangely soundless; her body is rigid. I come closer softly calling her name. Tears are running down her face and it is painful to watch her hold herself so quiet and taut.

I call her name a little louder

I keep saying her name, as I am afraid to touch her.

"Allory, honey it's Marc, wake up sweetheart.

"I am here. Please wake up."

Minutes go by, before she is less rigid. Finally, she slowly opens her eyes and sees me kneeling next to her bed. I carefully reach over and gently gather her to me as she cries soundlessly on my shoulder.

"I thought I was getting better," she whispers. "He is dead Marc, but he haunts me still."

Climbing into bed with Allory, I take her in my arms "You're safe with me tonight, sweetheart. Try to close your eyes and I will be here with you until morning."

I wake slowly the next morning with Allory snuggled against my side. I realize she slept the rest of the night without another nightmare.

I look down at her face as she is sleeping. I realize this courageous woman means everything to me.

Since Price did all those terrible things to her, I made a promise to myself that we will live a wonderful life as partners.

As I turn on my back, I see Allory slowly waking.

"Hi gorgeous, how did you sleep?" I ask as she opens her eyes.

"Pretty good after the nightmare," she tells me with a bright smile.

I am enslaved by the smile that lights up the room.

"Are you okay this morning after your nightmare?"

She thought a moment or two before answering.

"I am still a work in progress. Can you handle that until I find my way?"

"I love you and can't see past having you with me always."

Hiding her face in my neck for several moments. She wraps her arms around me tightly.

"You are my hero Allory, and I am crazy in love with you."

"Ok then! "She replies, lightening the mood. 'Let's get up showered and dressed and go find our future. I am feeling braver today."

"See you in a few. Dress casual I'll meet you downstairs, Allory."

When she comes into the kitchen, I tell her I am made her favourite blueberry pancakes as Sean gave me his secret recipe.

Sitting down next to me, she pours the coffee and takes two pancakes she slathers with butter and syrup.

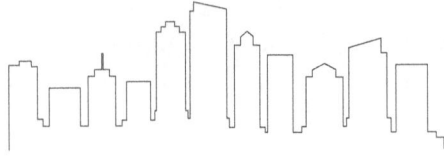

Chapter Fifty-Three

Over the next several weeks Marc, Jake and Connor have many meetings to bring their partnership to fruition.

Marc goes with me to my final appointment with Dr. Martin in late afternoon. She recommends I continue with the rehab exercises until I had no pain with full range of motion. She encourages me to continue to increase my range of motion and strength exercises in the pool.

The Zoom appointment with the counselor is more frustrating because I'm still having nightmares frequently. Her counselor reassured her that this is the way her subconscious is working through the trauma and fear.

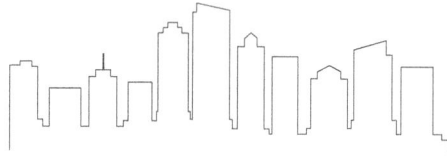

Chapter Fifty-Four

Marc has asked his brother Sebastian to assess real estate in Marseille that could accommodate the new branch of their security firm.

Marc continues to sleep with me each night and provides comfort when I wake from a nightmare. Over the next three weeks the episodes slowly reduce.

I begin to worry that Marc has not asked for our relationship to be more intimate. I know the relationship is solid. I feel silly that I can't just talk to Marc about what I want, in part because of Price and my injuries, but also because my confidence as a woman is at an all-time low.

I talk with my counsellor about my fears, and we come up with a plan to approach the topic with Marc.

Marc had been in all- day meetings today, so I plan a special but simple dinner I can prepare for tonight. I want more with Marc and I need to find a way to tell him that I am ready for an intimate relationship.

Checking the dinner one last time. I shower and change into a simple lavender dress and heels. I style my hair in a simple chignon and apply make-up.

When I come downstairs Marc is sitting in the living room reviewing a document. He looks up and smiles when I enter the room.

"How was your day, Allory?"

"Great! I went for a swim in the pool.

"I had a meeting with Aaron at UBC. Avery and I had lunch on the Westside. "Oh, and I made dinner for us tonight. All your favourites."

Marc looks at me with speculation.

"What is the occasion? You look gorgeous!"

"Just wanted to do something special for you today, you have been working so hard the last few days.

"Go through to the dining table. I will bring the food out."

I made pasta and salad, opening a Pinot Gris with dinner, asking Marc to pour the wine into the glasses.

"Wow, this is wonderful, Allory. Thank you." He raises his glass for a toast. "To us!".

Smiling, I take a sip of my wine.

"How was your day?"

"We are waiting on Sebastian to send his choices of real estate he has viewed as possible buildings for our new office. I want you to come with us when we go to Marseille."

"I would like that very much," I say before concentrating on eating.

"How was your appointment with the counsellor today?" he asks.

"It was very interesting. We talked about you and me," I say looking down at my plate.

When I look up. Marc has stopped eating and is staring at me.

"Let's finish our meal, then we can talk."

I tidy up after the meal and join Marc in the living room after refilling our wine glasses.

I sit down next to him on the sofa facing him. I am shy and tongue-tied for a few moments.

"So . . ." He draws out the word as he catches my gaze. "What did you talk to the counsellor about today that has you so nervous?"

I take a minute to calm my breath.

"We sleep together every night, but nothing else happens. I want to move our relationship to an intimate level. I am not sure that is what you want?"

Marc looks shocked. "Allory, I want that too, but I didn't want to rush you. You were hurt so badly. I didn't want to make things worse. What advice did the counsellor give you?"

"Thank God" I say with relief. "I thought you didn't want me anymore as I am damaged goods. The counsellor said go slow and do what feels right."

Marc leans over and takes my wineglass and sets it next to his on the side table.

He gently pulls me towards him and kisses me as I wrap my arms around his neck. It feels wonderful to be close to him.

When we come up for air, we smile at each other.

"Let's move this to the bedroom," Marc says as he releases me.

Grabbing my hand, he tugs me up off the sofa.

When we get upstairs, Marc leans down to turn the bedside lamp on. I sit down on the bed and slip off my heels.

"You are so beautiful and brave Allory. There is no rush. I want to make love to you and pleasure you. Stop me if anything doesn't feel right. It is just the two of us. I want us both to feel good."

Kneeling in front of me, he starts to unbutton the front of my dress. Then he pushes it off my shoulders, and I lift my hips, the dress slips off onto the floor.

I'm wearing a lacy black bra. Marc caresses my breast gently with his finger then traces my skin down my belly to the edge of the matching thong.

"So pretty," he whispers against my skin then lightly skims along my neck and shoulders with his lips and tongue.

Leaning back, I give him access, resting my weight on my shoulders. I shiver when he drops a kiss at the edge of my thong and retraces my skin with kisses until he reaches my neck. He gently bites down, and I gasp and meet his gaze.

"I'm less dressed than you," Brazenly asking him to join me naked.

"Getting there," he huffs out with a quiet laugh.

Standing up, he pulls his shirt over his head then undoes his pants and takes his boxers with them. He is gloriously naked, and I can't wait to touch him!

"Now who is overdressed, not for long, though," Marc says with a grin.

Reaching behind me he, unfastens my bra, he drags the straps down my arms, letting it drop on the floor. Next, he lifts my bottom, pulls my thong down my legs to join my bra.

His long fingers coast over my skin, he caresses down my neck, torso and legs leaving goosebumps along the way. He lowers me slowly down to the mattress while rearranging me in the process so there is room for him to lie next to me.

Capturing my gaze, he caresses my breast barely a handful for him. Stroking with one finger across my nipple until it is tight while repeating the action on my other breast before he sucks a nipple into his mouth and bites down. I gasp.

Yielding to the pleasure, he strokes my shoulders, arms, and torso, he dips a finger in my belly button. He then reaches down gently between my legs, and I am drenched. He softly strokes his finger over my clit, and I gasp.

Steadily, he touches me intimately, Marc slows his movements over my body. A jumble of thoughts is cascading inside me. Price gave me shame, took my power and painfully assaulted me. I felt dirty and used up. Marc is relentlessly, erasing those feelings replacing them with love and caring.

Marc makes me feel beautiful, freely giving his desire. He touches me with reverence.

I blindly focus on how he is kissing me while he separates my folds, gently he inserts a finger then a second.

Taking my hand, he wraps my fingers around his erection that is bumping up against my leg, I stroke him base to tip with increasing pressure.

I love we are both skin to skin.

I stroke him with increasing pressure with one hand. With the other hand I pet his chest molding the muscles as he catches his breath.

"I am not going to last baby. We need to use protection."

Leaning over me, fishing into his pant pocket for his wallet retrieving a condom package, ripping it open and rolling the condom on.

Kissing his way back up my body, he rubs his erection against my clit and sinks past my folds. I feel full.

He drops kisses along my neck at the same time he is pushing slowly inside me until I can take all of him.

This experience of caring and paying attention to me is new. As he starts gently thrusting in and out, I feel my orgasm almost there. He leans over and kisses me deeply, I come in a burst of feeling. He follows me shortly after.

Marc rolls to his side drawing me close to cuddle.

After a while, he rises from the bed and gets rid of the condom in the bathroom. He comes back with a warm washcloth and carefully cleans me up. I feel cherished as he returns to bed and pulls me into his arms.

"Love you Allory, you are mine to cherish," Marc's whisper brushing my ear.

"Love you too, Marc," murmuring before sleep claims me.

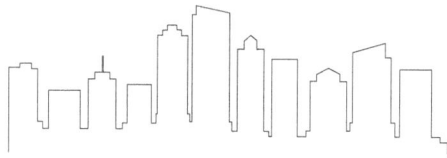

Chapter Fifty-Five

I watch Allory as she sleeps. I can't believe we have progressed so far that she was able to make love. I will do anything to keep her happy and safe. She has become my world. I close my eyes and sleep takes me quickly.

I wake in the dark. I hear Allory struggling. She is soundless, but her body is taut as a drawn bow. She is enmeshed in a nightmare.

At first, I think not to wake her, but she starts gasping for breath.

I gently shake her shoulder and whisper in her ear.

"Allory come back to me. It's Marc and I am holding you safe. I won't let anything harm you. Come on baby come back to me."

I keep talking to her until I see her eyelashes flicker open. She seems confused for a moment.

"Marc, thank God! Tell me Price is dead. He can't hurt me again."

"Yes, Allory, Price is dead, and he can never hurt you again. I am here and we will keep each other safe. Come back to me angel. I need you."

"You need me?"

"Yes, I need you. No one else can love me like you do. Please stay. Don't let the nightmares take you away from me. I am right here angel. Talk to me!"

Allory scoots up against the headboard and the last remnant of the nightmare leaves her eyes.

"I had hoped the nightmares would end now that you and I are together. Wishful thinking, I guess. My therapist warned me that they would not miraculously disappear, but I needed to be optimistic as I have come so far in the last few weeks.

"Aside from the damn nightmares I know I am doing better. I just hope I don't wake us each night or we won't get any rest. Maybe you should sleep in the other room."

"No way! I am staying with you, and we will get through this together.

"You are the most important person in my life, Allory.

"We stay together and support each other through nightmares and other challenges that life will bring us. You have come a long way already, don't give up. We will have a happy life together. I won't settle for anything less."

Allory throws her arms around me, and we fall on the mattress together. I cuddle her in my arms until she settles on her side. She is quiet for a long time until I realize she is softly snoring. I close my eyes drifting off to sleep. My last thought is that we will be okay.

Over the next weeks, Allory blossoms.

Aside from the office space for our business, I asked Sebastian to look for family homes for sale between our parents' winery and Marseille for Allory and her siblings to look at when they visit.

Allory's boss is so pleased with her work she has been doing in Vancouver he has promoted her to junior curator. She is looking forward to returning to work onsite at the museum again.

I will need a place in Vancouver for extended periods of time. I discussed real estate with Avery as she seems more in the know. We will likely buy a condo and rent it out when we are in France.

I close my computer and head out of the office. I am meeting Allory at the condo as it is movie night after our call to France.

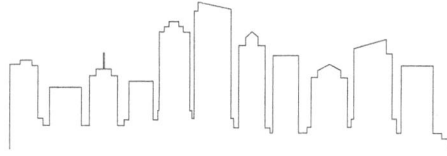

Chapter Fifty-Six
One Year Later

Marc and I are getting ready to land in Vancouver at the beginning of another spring. As I look out the airplane window the scene is much like I saw a year ago.

Recalling the whirlwind year we have had commuting between Vancouver and Marseille making the transition to spending part of the year in France, has been a good idea.

What makes me settled is to see Connor, Sean and Avery building thriving happy lives.

Connor comes and goes more than the rest of us do to manage his part-time law practice in Vancouver.

Connor's decision to buy our grandmother's Blind Bay estate when it came up for sale shouldn't have been a surprise to me. Recalling how much we all loved the estate and spent many happy hours there as children and youths. Connor wanted the house to stay in the family.

The four of us purchased a family home between Marc's parents' vineyard and our Marseille condo.

Marc's family has made us very much a part of their family. Avery spends a lot of time with Marc's mum, Julia as they both have a passion for interior design.

Sean has become thick as thieves with Marc's father, Antoine, and his brother Sebastian. Antoine is interested in Sean's building ideas, and Sebastian who is an architect, would like to consider a partnership with Sean. They are exploring the options available for both.

Connor, Marc, and Jake have become a tight trio with their business interests and partnership thriving. Connor loves the variety of his law practice doing both litigation and corporate law. The partnership between the three has worked out better than all of us could imagine.

Through all the business with Price and transitions in the last year, Marc remains my rock.

Unfortunately, I continue to have setbacks to my recovery, but recently, I'm having fewer flashbacks and nightmares, in part I believe because Marc has been with me each step of the way.

Restarting regular sessions with my French therapist when I am home in Marseille has helped my recovery. She fits well with me personally which I think is critically important. We have been working on resisting re-traumatization.

Marc and I have settled into his condo in Marseille which is close to work for both of us.

Céline was very happy when I came home to Marseille. We had a difficult time while I was in Vancouver connecting due to the time change and her frenetic workload. I am still amazed she flew to Vancouver to see me in the hospital although I have no memories of her being there.

Céline and our group of friends have seamlessly included Marc and his brother Sebastian into our gang. I have added a brother who teases me relentlessly like the rest of my expanded family that includes Jake.

Andre continues to be very pleased with my work on our partnership with UBC and has given me the lead in several initiatives with the university. It works for Marc and me to coordinate our work schedules to be in Vancouver at the same time.

Our time in Vancouver is now full of reconnecting with old friends and new. One of those people is Angel. I love spending time with Angel and her family.

Today as we arrive at the condo, I realize that Marc has been quiet during the drive from the airport.

"Are you tired? You seem quiet during the drive home."

"Just thinking. I have something special planned for us tonight."

"You going to give me a hint about that something special?"

"Nope, it's a surprise. You will just have to wait," he winks at me.

"Ok" I say grudgingly. "This had better be good," I say as we arrive at the underground parking. He replies, "Hope so!"

When we get upstairs, I order groceries and beverages for the next few weeks to be delivered. Then, going into our ensuite, I unpack, and shower. Marc joins me, so we run out of hot water.

I wear a dress in pretty shades of yellow with white sandals. Remembering it is spring in Vancouver I add a white cardigan to fend off the slight chill in the air. It was sunny and hot when we left France yesterday.

The delivery of groceries and beverages arrive when I go downstairs. I open a lovely Sauvignon Blanc from the box and pour two glasses of wine for Marc and me.

As, I'm putting the groceries away, Marc is coming down the stairs dressed in casual jeans and a soft white dress shirt.

"Man, my guy is handsome," I say as I reach up for a kiss prior to handing him his glass of wine.

Walking into the living room we glimpse the ocean through ceiling to floor windows. The sun is trying to peek through fluffy white clouds. To acclimatize to Vancouver time, we will try to stay up until after dinner as we had a decent snooze on our flight.

Sinking into the sofa, Marc and I snuggle together while we sip our wine.

Marc finishes his wine and sets my glass next to his on the table in front of us.

"Let's go for a walk it doesn't look cold outside but let's just take a light jacket in case." He gets our jackets from the hall closet.

Getting to street level, we naturally head toward the beach. The breeze is cool, but the sun is shining through the clouds. Marc holds my hand as we leisurely walk down the street.

The traffic is steady, we use a crosswalk to reach the beach side of the road. It is lovely outside with tall green trees along the walkway. Quaint shops on the other side of the street from us still open for a few more lingering hours to dusk.

Marc steers us to a forested area with lovely wrought iron benches and a beautiful spring garden in bloom. We sit down on a bench, and the fragrant smell of early blooms reaches me. From here, I can see a glimpse of Jericho Beach through the trees.

Turning to face me, Marc takes my hand.

"Allory, I live in awe of you every day--- for your resiliency, your strength, your huge heart, and your innate kindness. I thank you for picking me to be the guy in your life. I can't see a life without you.

"I thought long and hard about where to ask you the important question and finally decided I needed to ask you here where it all began.

"I want to make my life with you, share our families and add to our family. Will you be my wife, Allory? Love me, live with me, have a wonderful future?"

"Wow, that was some proposal, Marc!" Laughing, crying, kissing him passionately we come up for air.

As Marc waits for my answer, he looked nervous and excited at the same time. I can't leave him hanging.

"Yes, I will be your wife, live with you, grow our family together because we fought for our present and now a future. I love you Marc," kissing him until we are both breathless.

Marc reaches into his jacket pocket and pulls out a small blue box opening it so I can see. A beautiful half caret sapphire surrounded by diamonds. He slips the ring on my finger and places a gentle kiss overtop.

"It is beautiful, Marc," I say through the tears trickling down my cheeks.

Wiping my happy tears from face, he kisses me softly.

"I wanted to propose here in Vancouver but hope we can plan a wedding in Marseille or perhaps at my parents' vineyard.

"We could also have it at your family's home," he quickly adds, "whatever you want."

"I love your family, and I think it would make them very happy if we were married at the vineyard. Avery and your Mum will want to plan the whole thing. I have a few ideas but if it is okay with you, I would like to leave all the details to them.

"I'll plan the honeymoon," I add with a cheeky grin.

"Done and done," Marc replies with a gorgeous smile.

"On another note . . .surprise! The whole gang is here to help us celebrate our engagement. Avery and my mother have seen to the details. Since all of you love your Nana's estate, that is where the engagement party will be tomorrow night. All we need to do is show up on time and enjoy the party."

Dusk is casting shadows on the sidewalk as Marc, and I leave the beach and walk along Fourth Avenue. There is a wonderful neighbourhood pub we stop in for dinner before we go home to bed. Tomorrow will be a big and exciting day.

The fairies in our families had obviously been to our condo while we were out. I find a beautiful cream satin dress that Avery has chosen for me with matching shoes of sky blue. There is a tuxedo for Marc with shiny black shoes.

A beautiful invitation is lying on the foyer table giving the time and location of our engagement party.

"They are something else aren't they," I whisper to Marc. "How did we get so lucky?"

"Allory you deserve all that we can do for you. You are the centre of my world and crucial to my happiness, vital to Avery, Sean, and Connor's contentment. Never forget that!"

Hugging me tightly, before he leads us upstairs to our bedroom. We get ready for bed. When we climb under the covers in our huge comfy bed, Marc gathers me skin to skin.

We make love as if it is our first time. He explores me thoroughly, placing kisses over my lips, face, neck. Paying close attention to my breasts, belly and further down.

I kiss every inch of his skin I can reach. It is gentle and explosive at the same time. He has been so patient since the trauma allowing me to take the lead until I felt safe enough to let go. And best of all, he ensures we both enjoy our intimacy together.

This man has walked beside me every day after what Price did to me.

Lending his strength, shoring up my courage to deal with the trauma, prior rape and all my fears that I would never have a normal physical relationship.

His patience has won out. I am gifted with this wonderful man who treats me like I am whole even though some days I am not quite there. Demonstrating he will always wait for me to catch up. He is really the true gift. I fall asleep happy and smiling.

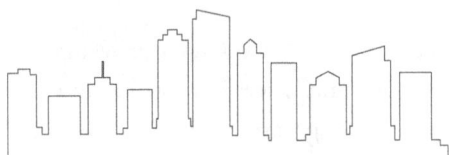

Chapter Fifty-Seven

I lie in bed as Allory falls asleep. I think tonight went well. Allory sometimes forgets that she has come so far since Price's death. Her nightmares are less frequent. She has been accepting of our physical intimacies and feels safe sharing her feelings openly.

She is excited about the engagement. I am so proud of this incredible woman as she stretches herself beyond her fears every day. I feel blessed that she has agreed to be my wife. I can't see my life without her now.

With that thought I drift to sleep gently clasping Allory's left hand.

I wake up rested, holding Marc's hand. Yesterday was a dream come true.

Sliding out of bed without waking Marc. I grab my robe and head to the kitchen to make our coffee and heat the croissants in the oven. I cut up fresh fruit to complete our breakfast. As I am setting the table Marc comes into the kitchen looking adorably ruffled. He is so handsome, I smirk. And he is all mine!

He leans over and gives me a delicious kiss.

"Good morning to you, my gorgeous man," I tease.

He gives me a wide grin as he pours our coffee. We bring the food and coffee to the table and sit across from each other. It is hard to stop smiling.

He takes a sip of coffee with much appreciation before grabbing a warm croissant from the plate.

"I want you to know we have a game plan for the party tonight. I don't want you stressing about the crowd. It is going to be as low key as we can make it."

"I knew you would think of everything. I just wish you didn't have to".

Sighing deeply, "I wish I didn't get panicky in crowds or enclosed spaces. I know it is because I was locked in a cell and then thrown in a container loaded with human cargo," I say ruefully.

"I hope over time this becomes less of a problem."

My therapist and I talk about it, but desensitization hasn't work so far.

"Allory, you have come light years from where you were last year. Give yourself some credit. I think you will be just fine. I have confidence in your resiliency, and I will be with you every step. We are a team, Chérie. Don't forget that.

"For now, we are going to have a leisurely morning. Get showered and dress casual for the car ride. Pack my suit, your dress, shoes and make up for the party and an overnight case because we will stay after the party at your Nana's house."

I relax once I have everything for the party and overnight stay in the car.

Suggesting we stop to have lunch at an ocean side pub in North Vancouver, Marc has factored in travel time. It is slightly warmer than yesterday with a gentle wind from the waterside making eating out on the patio enjoyable.

Because of the heavy traffic, we reach Nana's house at Lion's Bay in forty-five minutes. There were quite a few cars in the driveway when we arrive. Avery spots us from the entrance way and waves at me wildly.

The estate is ten acres of oceanfront with a long green lawn that runs from the house to the edge of the cliff above the ocean. Large cedar, maple, and west coast fir tower over the large mansion to provide shade in the afternoon. The house is designed to be open and airy.

Reminiscing, I draw on my many memories of my Nana, playing on the lawns as a child. She would set up elegant little tables so Avery and I could have afternoon tea with her. It seems fitting to celebrate Marc and I's engagement in this place I adored as a child.

Marc grabs our overnight bags, and I follow him with our party clothes and shoes into the house. He stops suddenly as he enters the house, I almost run into him as he looks around impressed.

Leading Marc upstairs to the second floor, I open the third door on the right. moving aside so he can put our luggage on the floor next to the bed.

There are fantastic drawings on the walls of fairies, and sprites.

"So, what do you think of my room?" I ask Marc with a huge grin.

He smothers a smile. "I didn't realize you were this whimsical!"

I flop on the bed. "Come join me Marc," I say with a laugh.

"No way. Then we will never leave this room and miss our party," he grins.

"Ok, I had to try," I say with a wink.

He grabs my hand and hauls me off the bed into the hallway. I see through the banisters that Connor and Sean have arrived, I race down the steps. I hug Sean tightly then Connor.

Marc is slower to descent the stairs and shakes hands with each of my brothers. Sean is having none of that and just grabs Marc for a hug.

"You are officially family now," Sean laughs.

Avery sticks her head out of the ballroom down the hall.

"Good you are all here. Come see what Julia and I have prepared for the party. I think Antoine and Sebastian are around somewhere too."

The ballroom is decorated in satins, the palest blue accented with a navy blue and white. Beautiful white tables dressed in blue accent laid with elegant tableware are grouped around a head table with enough distant I knew I wouldn't be claustrophobic.

Avery has hung a large blue and white satin sash on the wall with Marc and I's names and in smaller lettering congratulations.

"Oh Avery! This is all so beautiful. Thank you!" I walk over to give her a big hug.

"Look at your beautiful engagement ring!" sighing she takes my hand in hers.

"Yes, it is gorgeous," I say getting a bit teary.

"Nothing but the best for my baby sister.

"Now I want you and Marc to go for a walk on the estate grounds and just chill. Come back at four to shower and change.

"The guests will arrive around five. It won't be a crowd. Just close friends and family so you won't be overwhelmed. Everyone knows not to crowd you. We want you and Marc to enjoy this day."

"Ok, we will see you later." I grab Marc's hand and take him through to the back gardens.

The afternoon is warm, and a gentle ocean breeze is coming off the water. Marc and I take our time walking the estate until we come to a group of chairs overlooking the bay. We sit side by side just taking in the view and the peace of the estate.

At four o'clock we go back to our room, shower, and change. I apply make-up because there will be pictures and decide to leave my hair down after using the flat iron.

I look at Marc in his tuxedo so handsome I wish we didn't have to leave our room.

At five, we are ready to greet our friends, who are arriving to celebrate our engagement.

All friends and family, no enemies, no need to be afraid, I remind myself sternly.

I spy my uni friends with their significant others to the right of the ballroom door. I see Sebastian, Antoine, and Julia on the left with Julia's sister and her husband and two sons.

I see all the gang from Jake's office here in Vancouver including Angel, her two daughters and mother. Lastly, I see Avery, Sean, and Connor. I settle and begin to smile. I can do this.

Marc and I mingle. I am so happy to see so many people who care for us. No one crowds me. They come up one or two at a time just happy for me and Marc. I begin to relax. I know and care about everyone here.

The party goes into the wee hours and all the guests are given rooms for the night to avoid driving home in the dark. Avery has planned a buffet breakfast for everyone before they drive back to the city.

Marc's family will stay a week at Lion's Bay for a holiday before heading back to France. We will show Marc's family some of what we love about Vancouver before they return home. As for my uni friends we have already planned get togethers while Marc and I are in Vancouver.

Yesterday when Marc and I talked about the wedding we decided it would be held at the family vineyard in two months' time. That would allow us to meet our work commitments in Vancouver and ensure Sean, Connor, and Avery will be at our French home at the same time. Everything is falling into place.

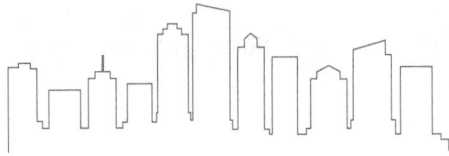

Chapter Fifty-Eight

The week following the engagement party, Marc and I are very busy with work commitments seeing each other only at breakfast and dinner. Each night, I fall into bed and sleep soundly. Every morning, I congratulate myself that I am getting better.

On Friday night I take the bus home. As I get off at my stop, I think I see a guy who looks like one of Price's associates getting off at my stop.

Scared, I turn left on the sidewalk to walk toward our condo. I look back to see the guy walking in the same direction as me.

I hurry into my building less than a block from where the bus drops me off. I get into the elevator. I see him coming into our building as the elevator door closes. I unlock the condo door and relock it behind me. I call Marc to explain what has happened. Maybe I am wrong about the guy?

Marc tells me that there are video cameras providing security to our block and he will review them at the office before he leaves. He is reassured I locked the door when I got home and would stay put until he arrives.

Making myself a cup of tea, trying to relax. I go through my calming exercises that my therapist and I developed. I feel my anxiety dissipate. I curl up with a blanket on the divan closing my eyes to rest until Marc comes home.

The dream that intrudes is one I have had many times.

I am back in that darkened room waiting for Price to return. Hurting badly and terrified for Price to come back. The dream changes. I hear my voice telling me wake up. Price is dead. I survived and this is just a bad dream.

Opening my eyes; it is still light outside. I hear the key in the door and see the security light disengage. Marc comes through the door purposely but slowly, assessing me. I sit up and give him a shaky grin.

Marc pulls me into a hug.

"I reviewed the security tapes. The guy who followed you off the bus doesn't fit the profile of any of Price's associates. It was just a case of mistaken identity baby. "You, okay?"

"I am better than okay. I fell asleep and the nightmare came but this time I changed the outcome. I knew it wasn't real. I remembered I survived and woke myself up. I think I am getting better Marc!"

"That is fantastic Allory. I always knew you were a fighter. The past harm Price did to you doesn't hold a candle to your strength and resiliency. This is huge victory today. Let's celebrate!"

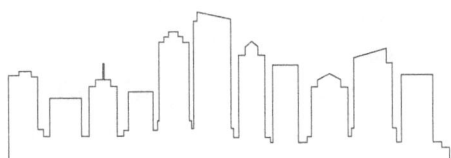

Chapter Fifty-Nine

Ever since that day, the nightmares have been less frequent. I can often wake myself now, which gives me a measure of control over the memories. I feel hope and look forward to what life can bring now, which is a far cry from how I viewed things a mere twelve months ago.

Today we're flying home to France—a few weeks after Marc and I got engaged—I'm looking out the window of the plane when I realize I have a huge smile on my face. For the first time in years, I can look back fondly at Vancouver, my home away from home. We are slowly making new memories there to replace the bad.

I ponder the coincidence that Marc and I were both touched by the darkness of human trafficking. Thinking about Marielle, I promise myself to honor her memory by living free.

I spend a few days when I come to Vancouver with Victim Services that rescue women from human trafficking. I also volunteer with a similar organization in Marseille. I do this in remembrance of Marielle, and all the women and children that never came home.

Running my hand down Marc' afternoon scruff, I kiss him full on the lips, with confidence. He looks at me enquiring what that kiss was for.

"Just because I can!"

I have a wedding to plan and a family to go home to.

◆ FriesenPress

One Printers Way
Altona, MB R0G 0B0
Canada

www.friesenpress.com

ISBN
978-1-03-831515-1 (Hardcover)
978-1-03-831514-4 (Paperback)
978-1-03-831516-8 (eBook)

1. FICTION, THRILLERS, CRIME

Distributed to the trade by The Ingram Book Company

www.ingramcontent.com/pod-product-compliance
Lightning Source LLC
LaVergne TN
LVHW042111140425
808599LV00002B/193